ALIEN HEARTS

GUY DE MAUPASSANT (1850–1893), journalist, novelist, poet, memoirist, playwright, and short-story writer, was one of the most notable men of letters of nineteenth-century France. He was born in Normandy to a middle-class family that had adopted the noble "de" prefix only a generation earlier. An indifferent student, Maupassant enlisted in the army during the Franco-Prussian War—staying only long enough to acquire an intense dislike for all things military—and then went on to a career as a civil servant. His entrée to the literary world was eased by Gustave Flaubert, who had been a childhood playmate of his mother's and who took the young man under his wing, introducing him into salon society. The bulk of Maupassant's published works, including nearly three hundred short stories and six novels, were written between 1880 and 1890, a period in which he also contributed to several Parisian daily newspapers. Among his best-known works are the novels *Bel-Ami* and *Pierre and Jean* and the fantastic tale "La Horla"; above all, he is celebrated for his stories, which transformed and defined the genre for years. In 1892, after attempting suicide to escape the hallucinations and headaches brought on by syphilis, Maupassant was committed to an asylum. He died eighteen months later.

RICHARD HOWARD was born in Cleveland in 1929. He is the author of fourteen volumes of poetry and has published more than one hundred fifty translations from the French, including works by Gide, Stendhal, de Beauvoir, Baudelaire, and de Gaulle. Howard received a National Book Award for his translation of *Fleurs du mal* and a Pulitzer Prize for *Untitled Subjects*, a collection of poetry.

ALIEN HEARTS

GUY DE MAUPASSANT

*Translated from the French
and with a preface by*

RICHARD HOWARD

NEW YORK REVIEW BOOKS

New York

THIS IS A NEW YORK REVIEW BOOK
PUBLISHED BY THE NEW YORK REVIEW OF BOOKS
435 Hudson Street, New York, NY 10014
www.nyrb.com

First published in *La Revue des deux mondes*, 1890

Library of Congress Cataloging-in-Publication Data
Maupassant, Guy de, 1850–1893.
 [Notre cœur. English]
 Alien hearts / by Guy de Maupassant ; translated and with an introduction
by Richard Howard.
    p. cm. — (New York Review Books classics)
 ISBN 978-1-59017-260-5 (alk. paper)
 I. Howard, Richard, 1929- II. Title.
 PQ2349.N713 2009
 843'.8—dc22

                          2009004537

ISBN 978-1-59017-260-5

Printed in the United States of America on acid-free paper.
10 9 8 7 6 5 4 3 2 1

CONTENTS

PREFACE

In 1890, three years before his death, the forty-year-old Guy de Maupassant, already suffering severe symptoms of the syphilis which would finally kill him, published *Alien Hearts* (*Notre Coeur*), his sixth novel ("finally kill him" because he had made three attempts to kill himself in order to escape the fate of his much younger brother Hervé, who after years of illness had died insane in 1889 in an asylum to which Guy himself had committed him).

Guy de Maupassant's career, at least as the world rapturously acknowledged it, was of course not as a novelist (though he was never a mediocre writer in any form he undertook—not only novels of great brilliance and power, but poetry, plays, travel narratives, journalistic chronicles, criticism) but as the author, in no more than a dozen years, of a remarkable number of what in English are called, rather precariously, *short stories*, starting in 1881 with "Boule de suif," his first fiction, or at least the first fiction that his mentor (and his mother's childhood friend) Flaubert, that tireless taskmaster, permitted him to sign with his own name. Three years later Maupassant had published as many as seventy *contes*, *nouvelles*, and what the journals of the day rather grandly called *chroniques littéraires*; in 1884 (the next year!) he published sixty new stories; in 1885 thirty more; in 1886 eighty more; in 1887, along with two novels, another twenty tales; but then, in the year before Hervé died, only eight stories; and in 1889, eight more; in the year after Hervé's death, *Alien Hearts* was published serially, and two plays were produced and successfully performed, and then not another word: after six weeks of uninterrupted crises (attacks of paralysis, spells of blindness), Guy de Maupassant died in Dr. Blanche's clinic in Passy. He was forty-three years old.

A year before this last completed novel appeared (though the sick man produced torsos of two others) in *La Revue des deux mondes*, for all its author's much publicized vows never to publish there (and never to become a member of the Académie Française, the latter vow sustained), Henry James, seven years Maupassant's senior, wrote an incisive study of the world-famous French author. Surely it is an evidence of "world fame" that two years after Maupassant's death, Tolstoy—to whom Turgenev had enthusiastically recommended the Frenchman's works—wrote an even more incisive study of those works, which now included *Alien Hearts*, though Tolstoy's critique was not merely incisive but left incisorial tooth marks: "In this last novel the author does not know who is to be loved and who is to be hated, nor does the reader know it, consequently he does not believe in the events described and is not interested in them."

Yet even if James *could* have included observations on Maupassant's last novel in that 1889 issue of *Harper's Weekly*, he was not likely to have dismissed it so witheringly; after all, it was in an essay of that same year that James had deplored "our Anglo-American mistrust of anything but the most guarded treatment of the great relation between men and women," in a defense of Maupassant so much more amiable than Tolstoy's contempt for the French writer's accounts of the "great relation." It is only to suggest the extent of Maupassant's celebrity that I cite the great Russian's judgment (I refer to Tolstoy—Turgenev was Henry James's "great Russian"); and after all, Tolstoy's declaration that the Frenchman did not know "who is to be loved and who is to be hated" is surely invidious—Maupassant knew (and revealed in all his writings, including this final novel) who is to be *pitied*, which must suffice even a Tolstoyan Christian in the effort to determine (and to communicate) who is to be loved.

Back in 1889, then, Henry James had not only anatomized Maupassant as far as Maupassant had exposed his corpus, he had also (a singular Jamesian achievement) successfully dramatized *The American,* his own melodramatic "Parisian" novel originally published in 1877, the very year he first met Maupassant at one of Flaubert's "Sundays." James was thirty-four then, Maupassant twenty-seven, and neither author in their various young productions had escaped criticism, from the company *chez* Flaubert and indeed elsewhere, for their evident innocence of the ways and wonders of *le gratin de Saint-Germain.* But by 1889 both men, in their entirely different ways, had become entirely conversant with Parisian high society, high life, high-handedness.

For example, thirteen years after his often-remarked and indeed remarkable characterization of Maupassant as "a lion in the path," Henry James published in 1903 a second and much more naturalized "Parisian" novel, *The Ambassadors,* which contains, as James himself pointed out, an "irrepressible outburst planted, stiffly and saliently, in the centre of the current, almost perhaps to the obstruction of traffic." This eruption is the "Live all you can" aria, spoken in Gloriani's (aka Rodin's) garden, an evident parallel to the aria which *Maupassant*'s version of Rodin (surnamed Prédolé) had performed (fourteen years earlier) quite as stiffly and saliently in the last chapter of part two of *Alien Hearts.*

James refers with a touch of embarrassment (in the 1909 New York Edition preface to *The Ambassadors*) to this "officious" discourse, perhaps because he writhes a little at his transfiguration of its "source" in the Maupassant novel written so long before. I indulge in all this tracing and tracking because Maupassant, in his own person (as I cite below in the rant from *Afloat*, a sort of nautical journal of reflections and observations published in 1888), makes such approving use of the rejection of worldliness and all its works in Prédolé's (Rodin's) boisterous credo. Though Henry James, I venture to guess, was not the least bit worried about the spiritual damage to which mundane society might or even must expose him, Guy de Maupassant saw things differently: his "heroine," Madame de Burne, the lady in whose salon the sculptor utters that credo, dismisses the Great Artist's idealistic lucubrations as "long-winded," and indeed most of the personnel of her fashionable salon is similarly put off by the Rodin figure and his curious table manners, as well as by his fanatical professionalism. As we read in *Afloat*, published the year before *Alien Hearts*:

> Anyone who wishes to maintain the absolute integrity of his thought and takes pride in the complete independence of his judgment in the observation of life, humanity, and the universe without prejudice, without preconceived notions and without religion, which is to say, without fear, must have nothing to do with what is known as society, for so contagious is the universal stupidity of this mundane world that he cannot frequent his fellow beings there, merely see and hear them, without in spite of himself becoming contaminated from all sides by their convictions, their ideas, their traditions, their superstitions and their prejudices which will inevitably oppress him with their customs and hypocrisy.

It is not the prophet Tolstoy who speaks thus, nor indeed the comfortably socialized American expat, but the preceptor of the salons Guy de Maupassant who writes his last novel, at least in part, in order to identify the debasements an aspiring spirit must confront upon venturing into the world of *mundane relations*; as a participating member of such a society he is compelled, at this culminating point in his career, to be not only its jester but its judge.

This may be a plausible moment at which to explain why the title of Maupassant's last completed novel appears, in English translation, as *Alien Hearts* rather than the obligatory but unserviceable *Our Heart*. During the agonizing months of 1890 Maupassant was so ill and in such physical pain that he could do nothing but work—on his last tales, on a play he completed but never saw performed, and on a second "society" novel which he regarded as a companion to *Notre Coeur* but of which he managed to complete only the first chapter; this work was to be called *Alien Souls*, and for reasons of thematic clarity, I have preferred the transposed version to the literal English translation of the titles of Maupassant's last "two novels."

The names of the characters in this circumstantially final novel deserve notice as well as the translated title of the book itself. It is striking that the inner circle of Madame de Burne's salon (they are all artists, writers, composers, philosophers, in accord with their flirtatious hostess's *salon taste*) have names whose initials, vowels, and sonorities echo those of the name *Guy de Maupassant*—from *Ma*riolle to *Ga*ston *de* La*ma*rthe, from *Ge*orges *de Ma*ltry to *Mas*sival, and even minor characters like Count *de Ma*rantin or the painter *de Mau*dol. Did the author multiply pseudonyms as if he wanted to examine himself under the surfaces of his characters, like Madame de Burne "anatomizing" herself in the huge three-panel mirror of her luxurious *cabinet de toilette*? In each of the characters designated by this onomastic puzzle is a possible double of Mariolle, detached and exaggerated to represent one of the contradictory tendencies that he feels increasingly at work within himself. As for Mariolle, the central character if not the hero, his name is obviously derived in part from *Mariolater*, a worshipper of the Virgin Mary; further, as the learned editors of one edition of *Notre Coeur* point out, in Italian slang a *mariolo* is a crook—hence *mariol*, an argot word for cunning, smart; and eventually *marionette*...

I'd like to add an explanatory note of my own here, though one somewhat remote from scholarship; contemporary American readers may be astonished to find that André Mariolle, who in even provisional lodgings is served by at least two domestics, who can afford to rent and recondition an entire villa and its garden to entertain his mistress when she consents to visit, and who is so securely accommodated on all financial occasions that he never needs to give a thought to what he can or cannot afford—this *rentier* does not have, in 1880, as the year is more or less indicated, a bathtub in his house, and when he gets ready to receive one of those cherished visits from Madame de Burne, he must go down the street to a (doubtless very nicely fitted) public baths to accomplish more than a whisk and a wipe. It is not so much a difference in the choices of cleanliness between the Anglo-American and Gallic leisure classes, I presume, as a difference in the modes of obtaining cleanliness—privacy, convenience, etc. Apparently Parisians way back then, say a century and some ago, managed things differently.

By his fortune, Mariolle is doomed, if not to a questionable ease of personal hygiene, to a dilettantism in all things save, in this final instance, matters of the heart. And even there, when one considers his management of Élisabeth in the last chapter, we are hard put to qualify his solution to his *peines de coeur* as anything but disastrous trifling. Maybe Tolstoy had more truth on his side than I was comfortable in according him at first glance. Certainly the novel shows to great advantage the natural analogy between André Mariolle's dilettantism and the "disenchanted" mobility of Madame de Burne; between Mariolle's artistic velleities and Madame de Burne's "constant and insatiable cravings for distractions," which Mariolle ends by finding "threatening." The two characters are the masculine and feminine faces of the most advanced modern psychological ruin (by which I mean they are extremely gifted and attractive in going about their mutual destruction), riven by analysis, devastated by doubts and pessimism, "confined by gnawing ironies": two faces which further contaminate each other, since Mariolle melts, empties, and sentimentalizes himself, while Madame de Burne increasingly loses the classic attributes of femininity. A kind of reciprocal contagion of the sexes is at work here.

Maupassant has obviously delayed the great sculptor's appearance in order to contrast the spiritual misery of Mariolle the emotional dilettante and the regrets of the writer Lamarthe, castrated by worldliness, to the serene power of the sculptor indifferent to manners, to affectations, to "futilities," and to all the Madame de

Burnes on earth: the Flaubertian artist committed to his art and coming to grips with substance, molding and caressing matter exclusively. For all the training Maupassant received from the Master, was he not aware that he would never be apt to achieve such a condition? One French scholar has astutely analyzed Maupassant's development as a writer, though hardly his achievement: "increasingly, the sentence tends to become the paragraph, the paragraph—quite monotonously—becomes the page, and the final impression is that of a void of suffering through which wanders a wave of sound and interminable complaint."

—RICHARD HOWARD

ALIEN HEARTS

PART ONE

I

A day came when Massival—the musician, the famous composer of *Rebecca*, the man who for at least fifteen years had been called "our distinguished young maestro"—asked his friend André Mariolle, "Why the devil haven't I ever seen you at Michèle de Burne's? If you ask me, she's one of the most...interesting women in Paris. In today's Paris, at any rate."

"Because I don't consider myself likely to fit in with those—with her set."

"You're making a mistake, my friend. As salons go, hers is a real original: not at all old-fashioned, quite lively, actually rather ...artistic. The music is excellent and the talk as good as old du Deffand's scandal ever was. You'd be more than welcome there—for one thing, you play the violin to perfection; for another, people say good things about you, and besides, you have a reputation for being 'unusual' and rather hard to get."

Flattered but still reluctant, and suspecting that the young woman in question was quite aware of this determined overture, Mariolle shrugged, "Not my sort of thing." Yet his intended rejection was mingled with an already perceptible consent.

Massival went on. "Come with me one of these days. I'll introduce you—besides you already know her from hearing so much about her. She's a very pretty woman, and remarkably intelligent. I don't think she's thirty, but she won't marry again—she had a bad time with the first one. So she's made a salon where you meet interesting types—not the usual smart lawyers or dumb dukes.

Just enough of those to give it a touch of class. I know she'd be pleased if I brought you along."

Won over, Mariolle answered, "All right then, one of these days."

And early the following week the composer dropped by with a question: "Are you free tomorrow night?"

"I could be... I suppose so."

"Fine. Then you're coming with me to Madame de Burne's for dinner. She's asked me to invite you—I even have a note from her for you."

After a few seconds' hesitation for form's sake, Mariolle replied, "All right, I'll come."

At thirty-seven André Mariolle, unmarried and without profession, rich enough to live as he pleased, to travel where he liked, and to collect a houseful of modern paintings and old porcelain, passed for a witty fellow, rather whimsical, rather willful, rather superior, who affected solitude for reasons of pride rather than shyness. Talented and astute but lazy, likely to understand everything and even to accomplish something, he had nonetheless been content to enjoy life as a spectator, or rather as an amateur. Had he been poor, he would doubtless have become remarkable, or at least famous; born to wealth, he endlessly reproached himself for turning into a nobody. Of course he had made several halfhearted gestures in the direction of the arts: one toward literature, publishing some notably "stylish" travel sketches; another toward music, studying the violin and gaining recognition, even among professionals, as a really talented amateur; and one toward sculpture, an art in which an original approach, a talent for suggesting bold and convincing figures replaces, in the eyes of the ignorant, any amount of study and knowledge. His terracotta statuette, *Tunisian Masseur*, had even received some attention in last year's Salon.

A fine horseman, he was also said to be an expert fencer, though he never exhibited his skill in public, here too yielding to the same anxiety which kept him from frequenting circles in which there might be serious competition.

But his friends appreciated his talents and praised him to the skies, perhaps because he never sought to eclipse any of them. Everyone agreed he was a loyal friend and a congenial companion, a thoroughly likable fellow.

Taller than average, he wore his black beard clipped short and carefully pointed at the chin, his close-curled hair slightly grizzled at the temples; his clear brown eyes were bright, mistrustful, and a little hard.

His closest friends were artists, the novelist Gaston de Lamarthe, the composer Massival, the painters Jobin, Rivollet, and Maudol, all of whom seemed to set great store by his friendship, his wit, and even his judgment, though actually, with the vanity inseparable from public success, they regarded him as an amiable and quite intelligent failure.

His air of lofty reserve seemed to say, "I'm nothing because I choose not to do anything." Consequently he moved in a tight little circle, scorning elegant flirtations and the grand salons where all eyes were on others who would have outshone him, casting him into the ranks of worldly supernumeraries. He made his appearances only in houses where his serious and undisclosed talents were sure to be acknowledged; and if he had so readily consented to be introduced to Madame Michèle de Burne, it was because his best friends, those who everywhere proclaimed his hidden virtues, were this young woman's intimates.

She lived in a pretty entresol in the rue du Général Foy, behind the church of Saint-Augustine. Two rooms faced the street: the dining room and a salon for large parties. Two others opened onto a splendid garden that belonged to the building's owner: the first of these was a second salon, longer than it was wide, with three windows overlooking the trees that brushed the shutters. This room contained rare objects and splendidly simple pieces of furniture, evidence of sober taste and limitless means. The chairs, the tables, the charming cabinets or étagères, the pictures, the fans and figurines behind glass, the vases, the huge escutcheon in the middle of one panel—everything in this young woman's apartment attracted or held the attention by its form, its date, or its elegance. To create this interior, of which she was almost as proud as of her own person, Madame de Burne had drawn on the knowledge, the friendship, and the knowing eye of every artist she knew. To please a young woman who was so rich and who paid so generously, they had ransacked Paris for objects over-looked by the average collector, and with their complicity she had made a famous and exclusive interior where she liked to think her guests had a better time and returned more readily than to the conventional salons of any other hostess in Paris.

It was, in fact, a favorite theory of hers that subtly shaded hangings and fabrics along with comfortable chairs and couches, harmonizing in outline and gracefully grouped, must captivate a visitor and put him at ease quite as much as the loveliest smiles. Whether rich or poor, she would say, sympathetic or disagreeable rooms attract, retain, or repel even as the beings who inhabit them. They enliven or benumb the heart, warm or chill the mind, encourage conversation or impose silence, awaken gaiety or sad-ness, and ultimately give each guest an unconscious desire to re-main or to depart.

In the center of this rather dimly lit gallery, between two elab-orately planted jardinieres, a grand piano held a place of honor, dominating everything else in the room. At the far end, tall dou-ble doors opened onto the bedroom, beyond which was a large and elegant boudoir, hung with flowered chintz that made the place a sort of garden, where Madame de Burne might usually be found when she was alone.

Married to a well-bred monster, one of those domestic tyrants who brook no resistance, she had, at first, been very unhappy. For five years subjected to the demands, the tempers, the jealousies, even the physical abuse of an intolerable master, terrified and be-wildered, she never once protested at this revelation of conjugal life, crushed beneath the tormenting and despotic will of the bru-tal creature whose prey she had become.

One evening, on his way home, he died of a ruptured aneurysm; and when the body, wrapped in a sheet, was carried into the apartment, all she could do was stare at it, transfixed, not believing the reality of her deliverance, overcome by a transport of repressed joy that she was terrified to reveal.

By nature independent, gay, even exuberant, seductively responsive and given to those spontaneous sallies that sparkle in the conversation of certain daughters of Paris who seem to have inhaled since childhood the pungent breath of the boulevards laden with the nightly laughter of audiences leaving the theaters, Madame de Burne's five years of bondage had nonetheless endowed her with a singular timidity which mingled oddly with her youthful mettle, a great fear of saying too much, of going too far, along with a fierce yearning for emancipation and a firm resolve never again to compromise her freedom.

A man of the world, her husband had trained her to receive his guests like an elegant slave, perfectly dressed and perfectly mute. Among this despot's friends were a number of artists whom she had welcomed with curiosity and listened to with pleasure, never daring to reveal how well she understood them, how much she appreciated their conversation.

Her mourning over and done with, an evening came when she invited several of these men to dinner. Two sent regrets, three accepted and were astonished to find a young woman of open mind and beguiling wit who immediately put them at their ease, declaring with graceful candor how much pleasure they had given her by coming to her house in days gone by.

And gradually, among the old acquaintances who had ignored or misread her, she made a choice according to her own tastes and ended by receiving, as a young widow and a free spirit—though determined to remain quite untouched by scandal—many of the most sought-after men in Paris, and several women as well.

The first to be admitted became intimates, the regulars who attracted others, giving her house the atmosphere of a little court where each habitué contributed a talent or at least a title, for several carefully selected aristocrats mingled with these cultivated commoners.

Her father, Monsieur de Pradon, who occupied the apartment above her own, served as a formidable chaperon: an elegant and well-spoken old beau, he danced attendance on this splendid creature whom he treated as a great lady rather than a daughter, presiding over her Thursday dinners which were soon much talked about in Paris and invitations to which were eagerly sought. The claims of these would-be guests were discussed and frequently rejected after a sort of vote by the inner circle. Clever remarks made at these dinners were repeated all over town, and the debuts of young musicians at Madame de Burne's became a sort of baptism by gossip. A long-haired "poet of genius" introduced by Gaston de Lamarthe would replace the Hungarian violinist brought by Massival, and more than one "exotic dancer" offered her frantic poses here before going on at l'Eden or the Folies Bergère.

Madame de Burne, jealously guarded by her friends and retaining a disagreeable recollection of the world at large from her passage through it under marital supervision, wisely chose not to enlarge her circle of acquaintances to any great extent. Content with her life and at the same time fearing the tongue of scandal, she indulged her mildly bohemian tendencies with an altogether bourgeois prudence. She prized her reputation, curbed any unconsidered impulse, and remained correct in her caprices, moderate in her audacities. No one had reason to suspect any flirtation, any affair, any secret.

Each of the regulars had attempted to seduce her; none, it was said, had succeeded. They admitted as much, confessed their failure with some surprise, for no man is willing, perhaps with some reason, to acknowledge the virtue of an unattached woman. The story went that early in their conjugal relations her husband had behaved with such disgusting brutality and made such unheard-of demands that she had been permanently "cured" of the love of men. There was a good deal of discussion about this likelihood among the inner circle, and the preponderant opinion was that a girl raised in a fantasy of future tenderness, in the expectation of a wondrous mystery imagined as indecent and faintly impure but distinguished for all that, must remain permanently scarred by a boorish disclosure of marital demands.

The worldly philosopher Georges de Maltry chuckled and prophesied: "Her time will come. It always does for women like that. The longer it takes, the worse it will be. Given her tastes, she'll most likely fall in love with a pianist . . . or some tenor."

Gaston de Lamarthe had other ideas. A novelist by profession, an observer, and indeed a psychologist specializing in the study of high society from which he drew portraits as ironic as they were recognizable, he claimed to know women and to analyze them with a unique and infallible penetration. Madame de Burne he classified among contemporary neurotics whose type he had anatomized in his interesting novel *One of the Brood*. He had been the first to describe this new race of women tormented by a sort of rational hysteria, solicited by a thousand contradictory longings which never manage to reach the level of real desires, disillusioned by everything without having attempted anything because of frustrations of the period—fashionable dilemmas, problems of the modern novel—and who, without ardor, without appetites, seem to combine the whims of a spoiled child with the dismissiveness of an old cynic.

He had failed, like the others, in his attempts at seduction.

For all the loyal members of the group had fallen, one after the next, in love with Madame de Burne and, after the crisis, had remained attentive and fond to various degrees. Gradually they had formed a sort of sect, a *chapelle ardente* of which she was the Madonna, endlessly invoked, her powerful spell cast even at some distance. They celebrated her, bragged about her, criticized her, and belittled her according to the rancors, the favors, the irritations, or the preferences she had daily displayed. Continually jealous of one another, continually spying on one another, and above all closing ranks around her in order to prevent some more likely rival from approaching, there were seven intimates: Massival, Gaston de Lamarthe, portly Fresnel, the worldly young philosopher Georges de Maltry, famous for his paradoxes, his eloquent and elaborate erudition, so up-to-the-minute that he was quite incomprehensible to even his most fervent admirers, as well as for his taste in clothes which was as far-fetched as his theories. Madame de Burne had added to these happy few several worldly types known to be clever—the Count de Maratin, Baron de Gravil, and two or three more.

The two most privileged members of this elite battalion appeared to be Massival and Lamarthe, who apparently possessed the gift of endlessly amusing the young woman by their bohemian manners and their skill at making fun of everyone present, even their hostess when she would put up with it. But her natural or conscious concern never to show a prolonged and marked predilection to any one of her admirers, her cool and mocking coquetry, and the genuine equity of her favor maintained among them a sort of friendship spiced with hostility and an intensity of spirit which kept them alert.

Occasionally one of them, to vex the others, would introduce a friend. But since such a friend was never a very eminent or very interesting figure, the others soon joined forces to drive him out.

This was how it happened that Massival brought his friend André Mariolle to the house.

A servant wearing a black coat announced the names: "Monsieur Massival! Monsieur Mariolle!"

Under a huge silk lampshade shedding a pink cloud on a square table of antique marble, the heads of one woman and three men were bent over an album Lamarthe had just brought. Standing in front of them, the novelist was turning the leaves, commenting on the pictures.

One of the heads looked up, and Mariolle, as he stepped forward, saw a bright face, the reddish-blond hairs at the temples glowing as if on fire. The delicate turned-up nose seemed to keep the face smiling; the clearly outlined lips, the deep dimples of the cheeks, the rather prominent cleft chin gave it a teasing look, while the eyes, in strange contrast, were tinged with sadness. They were pale blue, as if they had been washed, scrubbed, and faded, and the dark pupils gleamed at the center, round and dilated. This singular and brilliant luster of the eyes seemed to betray dreams of morphine, or perhaps merely the coquettish application of belladonna.

Madame de Burne stood up and, holding out her hand, thanked the visitor for coming. "I began asking our friends to bring you here long ago, but I always have to beg and beg again for such things before they happen."

She was tall and elegant, her gestures rather deliberate, her modest décolletage revealing only the tops of her fine shoulders under the pink lamplight. Yet her hair was not red after all, merely the untranslatable color of certain dying leaves inflamed by autumn.

Then she introduced Monsieur Mariolle to her father, who bowed and offered his hand.

The men, in three groups, were chatting among themselves, seeming quite at home, as if they were in a sort of club where a woman's presence compelled a certain delicacy of manner.

Count de Marantin was talking to Fresnel, whose assiduous visits to the house and Madame de Burne's evident fondness for him frequently irritated her friends. Still young but portly as a judge, puffy and beardless, his skull vaguely haloed by bright downy hairs, he was a common-looking man and rather tedious, and probably had only one virtue for his hostess, disagreeable to the others but essential in her eyes, that of loving her blindly, more deeply than all the rest. They had nicknamed him "the Seal." A married man, he had never even mentioned introducing his wife, who was said to be extremely jealous, from a distance, of the young widow. Lamarthe and Massival were especially annoyed by the cordiality she showed this puffy rival, and when they couldn't refrain from expressing this lamentable taste of hers, selfish and vulgar as it was, she would answer with a smile, "I love him like a good, faithful cocker spaniel."

Georges de Maltry was telling Gaston de Lamarthe about the latest and still-disputed discovery in microbiology. He elaborated on the subject endlessly, and the novelist responded with the enthusiasm with which men of letters welcome anything that strikes them as original and new.

The tall, slender, flax-blond philosopher of the high life was encased in a suit fitting very close around his hips. His delicate head emerged from the high white collar, pale under the flat blond strands which seemed pasted on his skull.

As for Lamarthe—Gaston de Lamarthe, whose grammatical particle had inoculated him against certain worldly pretensions— he was first and foremost a man of letters, a pitiless and terrible man of letters. Armed with a photographic memory for images, attitudes, and gestures, and endowed with a born novelist's nose for character flaws, he stored up copy from morning to night. He had a clear perception of forms and an instinctive sensitivity to weakness, and with these two simple senses he imparted to his books the color, the tone, the movement of life itself: they appeared to consist of hunks of human life torn from reality. Agitations, suppositions, delight, and rage broke out on the publication of his novels, for people always imagined they recognized prominent figures only faintly protected by a transparent mask. Thus Lamarthe's progress through the salons of Paris left a froth of anxieties in his wake, especially since he had also published a volume of "intimate" memoirs in which many of his acquaintances had been portrayed without obvious malevolence but with a precision and severity that inevitably left them feeling drawn and quartered. Someone once nicknamed him "Friends, Watch Out!" A cold heart and an enigmatic soul, he was said to have been madly in love, long ago, with a woman who had made him suffer, and to have taken subsequent revenge on the rest of the sex.

Massival and he were on the best of terms, but the musician

was of an altogether different nature, more expansive, less tormented perhaps, but evidently more sensitive. After two great successes, a work performed in Brussels and then brought to Paris where it had been acclaimed at the Opéra Comique, then a second work immediately accepted and put on at the Grand Opéra itself and received as the promise of a splendid talent, he had suffered the kind of setback which strikes so many contemporary artists—a sort of precocious paralysis. Rather than growing old in fame and success like their fathers, they seem threatened with impotence in the prime of life. Lamarthe used to say, "Today there are only aborted great men in France."

It was Massival's turn to be very much in love with Madame de Burne, and the group could talk of little else. All eyes turned toward him when, with an adoring glance, he kissed her hand. "Are we late?" he asked.

"No, not at all. I'm still expecting Baron de Gravil and the Marquise de Bratiane."

"Ah, wonderful, the marquise! So we'll have some music this evening."

"I certainly hope so."

Whereupon the latecomers arrived. The marquise—a vivacious woman of Italian origin, a little too short because she was slightly hunchbacked, with black eyes, black lashes, black eyebrows, and even black curls, so thick that they invaded her forehead and threatened her eyes—was said to have the finest voice in society. The baron, a proper gentleman with a hollow chest and a huge head, was not entirely present without his cello in his hands. A passionate music lover, he frequented only those houses where music was a principal entertainment.

Dinner was announced, and Madame de Burne, taking André Mariolle's arm, let her guests precede her. The two of them remained behind in the salon, and as they began to follow the others, she shot him a sidelong glance of her pale eyes with their glistening black pupils. Suddenly he perceived a more complex mind and a more searching interest than is usually manifested by an attractive hostess receiving an ordinary guest at her table for the first time.

The dinner was a little dull, monotonous in fact. Lamarthe, all nerves, seemed hostile to everyone, not openly hostile, for he was careful to seem polite, but armed with that almost imperceptible animosity which lowers the social thermometer. Massival, preoccupied and silent, ate little and stared at his plate, glancing occasionally at his hostess, who appeared to be in another place altogether. Inattentive, smiling in reply to amusing remarks, then suddenly serious, she seemed that evening to have something on her mind that was much more important than her friends. She performed her duties as a hostess to the marquise and to Mariolle, but mechanically, as if indifferent to both her house and herself. Fresnel and Maltry began to quarrel about modern poetry—the former possessing the commonplace opinions of the ordinary man of the world, and Maltry the usual impenetrable perceptions of the more ingenious versifiers. Several times during this dinner, Mariolle again encountered his hostess's searching glance, but vaguer now, less fixed, less curious. Only Marquise de Bratiane, Count de Marantin, and Baron de Gravil continued their discussion at the table, dusting off a great variety of topics.

Later in the evening, Massival, increasingly depressed, sat down at the piano and touched a few notes. Madame de Burne seemed to be reborn, and quickly organized a little concert of the pieces she loved most. The marquise was in voice, and stimulated by Massival's presence, she sang like a true artist. The musician accompanied her with that melancholy countenance he always assumed when performing. His hair, which he wore long, brushed his coat collar, mingled with the lustrous curls of his beard. Many women had loved this man and pursued him still, it was rumored. Madame de Burne, seated near the piano, listening intently, seemed at once to be contemplating him and not to see him, and Mariolle was slightly jealous. Not particularly jealous on account of her and of him; but at the sight of this woman's gaze fixed on such an Illustrious Personage, his masculine vanity was humiliated by the thought of how She might classify him according to the amount of fame achieved. It was not the first time he had secretly suffered from encountering famous men in the presence of women whose favor is for many the supreme recompense of success.

At about ten o'clock there arrived, one after the other, Baroness de Frémines and two opulent Jewesses. There was much talk of a wedding announced and a divorce anticipated.

Mariolle observed Madame de Burne, now seated under a bronze column that supported an enormous lamp. Her delicate nose with its turned-up tip, the dimples in her cheeks, and the slight fold of flesh that divided her chin made her look like a mischievous child, though she was nearing thirty and the faded-flower expression of her eyes gave her face a sort of disturbing mystery. Her skin, under the bright light, had the texture of pale velvet, while her hair glowed with russet highlights whenever she moved her head.

She felt Mariolle's gaze from the other end of the salon, and standing up, walked toward him, smiling, as though in answer to a call. "You must be a little bored, monsieur," she murmured. "The manners of a strange house are always boring."

He protested. She took a chair and sat down beside him. At once they began to talk. It was instantaneous with each of them, like a fire catching at the touch of a match—as if they had communicated their opinions, their sensations to each other in advance, as if the same nature, the same education, the same tastes had predisposed them to understand each other and destined them to meet.

Perhaps there had been some adroitness on the young woman's part, but what impressed Mariolle was the pleasure of finding someone who listens, who understands, who responds. Flattered by her welcome, enchanted by the provocative grace she knew how to show her guests, he made every effort to reveal that hidden turn of mind, so personal, so delicate, which won him, when it was perceived, such rare and lively sympathy. All of a sudden she declared, "How lovely it is to have a conversation with you, monsieur. Of course I'd been told it would be."

He felt himself blush and said quite boldly, "While I'd been told, madame, that you were—"

She interrupted him. "Something of a coquette? I often am, with people I like. Everyone knows it, and I don't deny the fact, but you'll find that my coquetry is quite impartial, which allows me to keep my friends. I never lose a friend." There was a strange tone in her voice, as if she were telling him to keep calm and not assume too much: "Don't be deceived—you won't get any more than the rest."

"You're warning me of the dangers that lie in my path, aren't you? Thank you, madame. I'm grateful."

She had given him an opportunity to speak about her; he seized it. First he paid her compliments and realized that she enjoyed them; then he roused her curiosity by telling her what he had heard about her in the various circles he moved in. A little anxious, she could not conceal her desire to hear, though she affected a great indifference as to what people might think of her existence and her tastes.

He painted a flattering portrait of an independent, intelligent woman, superior and seductive, who had surrounded herself with distinguished men yet remained an accomplished woman of the world. She protested, smiling and uttering little "noes" of contented egoism, vastly entertained by the details he was furnishing, and in a playful tone insisted on hearing more, questioning him with a sensual appetite for flattery.

As he observed her, he thought, "Really, she's nothing but a child, like all the rest." And he turned a pretty phrase in which he praised her genuine love of the arts, so rare in women.

At which her tone changed to an unexpected sort of teasing, that broad French mockery that seems the very essence of our nation. Mariolle had overdone it. She showed him that she wasn't taken in. "Good Lord," she said, "frankly I'm not sure if it's the arts I love, or the artists!"

"And how could you love the artists without loving the arts?"

"Because sometimes they're more fun than the men one meets in . . . the world."

"Yes, but they have more inconvenient defects."

"They certainly do."

"Then you don't much care for music?"

"Excuse me, I love music. I think I love music most of all. Even though Massival believes I don't understand a thing about it."

"He's told you that?"

"No, but that's what he believes."

"How do you know?"

"Oh, women can guess almost everything they don't know."

"And Massival believes you don't understand anything about music?"

"Of course. I can tell just by the way he explains things to me, the way he underlines the subtleties, as if he's thinking, 'It's no use, I'm only doing this for you because you're nice and I like you.'"

"Well, you know, he told me I could hear better music here than in any other house in Paris."

"Yes, thanks to him."

"And literature—you don't care much for that?"

"Oh, I do. Certainly I do. I even imagine I understand what I read, in spite of what Lamarthe says."

"Who also says you don't understand what you read. . . ?"

"Of course."

"But who also hasn't told you as much. . . ?"

"Oh no, he's told me. He claims that certain women may have an accurate perception of certain sentiments—of the truth of characters, of psychology in general, but that they're totally incapable of discerning what's superior in his profession, by which he means the art of literature. When he pronounces that word, 'art,' there's no enduring him."

"And what's your opinion of the matter, madame?" asked Mariolle with a smile.

She reflected for a few seconds, then met his eyes to see whether he was likely to understand what she would say. "I have my ideas on the subject. I believe that sentiment—feelings, you know—can make a woman's mind grasp anything, only it doesn't always stay. Do you know what I mean?"

"No, not quite, madame."

"I mean that in order for us to understand as men do, you must appeal to us as women before addressing our intelligence. We aren't interested in what a man tells us unless he gains our sympathy first, for we see everything through feeling. I'm not saying through love—no, through feeling, which takes all kinds of forms... manifestations, nuances. Feeling is what belongs to us, and you don't really understand it because it... it *darkens* you, while it illuminates us. Oh, I know this all sounds very vague. I can't help it! Look, if a man loves a woman and she cares for him, she has to feel loved in order to be capable of that kind of effort, and if this man is a superior person, he can—if he takes the trouble—he can make a woman understand anything, he can communicate, at certain moments and at certain points, his entire intellect. Oh! I know it often disappears afterward, it fades away, for we forget. Oh! we forget—the way air forgets the words we speak. We're intuitive and... illuminable, but so variable, so impressionable, we're changed by whatever surrounds us. If you knew how often I go through states of mind that make me a different woman, different according to the time of day, and how well I feel and what I've been reading and what I've been told... There are days when I have the soul of a blameless mother of a family, only without children, and others when I have the soul of a cocotte, only without lovers."

Charmed, Mariolle asked, "And do you believe that most intelligent women are capable of this intellectual activity?"

"Yes, I do. Only they're asleep—it's dormant in them—and besides, they lead the kind of life that drags them one way or another..."

He asked again, "And you really prefer music to the other arts?"

"Yes, I do. But what I was telling you just now is so true! I know I wouldn't have enjoyed it so deeply, loved it the way I do, if it weren't for that wonderful Massival. All the works of the great composers that I used to love so passionately on my own, why, he's given them a soul by showing me how to play them. It's really too bad he's married!"

She uttered these last words playfully, but at the same time with a deep regret that overwhelmed both her theories about women and her own admiration for the arts.

It was true, Massival was a married man. He had committed himself long before the days of his success to one of those marriages a man drags through fame to his dying day. Moreover he never mentioned his wife, she never accompanied him on his sorties into society, and though he had three children, the fact was virtually unknown.

Mariolle burst out laughing. No doubt about it, the woman was a delight, so different from anything he had expected, from anything he knew, and extremely pretty as well. He stared, with an insistence that didn't seem to bother her, at this rather defiant face, at once so gay and so grave, with its bold nose and its sensual coloring, the soft warmth of her skin, flushed by the full summer of a maturity so new, so tender, so delicious that she seemed to have reached the year, the month, the very moment of her complete fulfillment as a woman. He wondered, "How much makeup is she wearing?" and he searched for the telltale line, darker or lighter, at the roots of her hair, without being able to find it.

Muffled footsteps on the carpet behind him made him start and turn his head. Two servingmen were carrying in the tea table. The little blue flame of the alcohol lamp made the water murmur in a big silver vessel as complicated and shiny as a chemist's apparatus.

"You'll have some tea?" she asked. When he had accepted, she stood up and walked straight over to the table where the steam was singing in the belly of this machine, amid a spread of cakes, cookies, candied fruit, and bonbons. And as her profile was outlined against the pale hangings of the salon, Mariolle observed the delicacy of her waist and the grace of her hips beneath the broad shoulders and the full breasts he had admired earlier. As the bright gown trailed behind her and seemed to extend an endless body over the carpet, he said to himself, crudely enough, "A mermaid, no, a siren! Everything about her is alluring!" She was moving now between her guests, offering refreshments with graceful gestures. Mariolle stared after her, but Lamarthe, who was walking along with his cup in one hand, came up to him and said, "Shall we leave together?"

"Certainly."

"Right away, if it's all the same to you."

They left the house. In the street, the novelist asked, "Are you going home or to the club?"

"I'll stop in at the club for an hour."

"Les Tambourins?"

"Yes."

"I'll drop you off, but I won't go in. Those places bore me. I belong just to get a carriage." He took Mariolle's arm and they walked past the church of Saint-Augustine.

A few steps on, Mariolle said, "What a strange woman! What do you make of her?"

Lamarthe laughed aloud. "Now it begins," he said. "You're catching it, just like all the rest of us: I'm cured now, but I had the disease, and I recognize the symptoms. The crisis consists of talking about her—nothing but her—whenever her friends meet, wherever they find each other..."

"Well, it's only natural for me—it's my first time and I scarcely know her."

"All right. We'll talk about her. Believe me, you'll fall in love with her. It's inevitable—everyone does."

"She's as seductive as all that?"

"Yes and no. Men who like old-fashioned women, women with a soul, with a heart, with sensibility—you know, the women in old novels—can't stand her; they get to loathe her so much they end up saying terrible things about her. Those of us who like something modern—well, we have to admit she's wonderful, provided you don't get involved. And that's precisely what you do. Oh, nobody dies of it, you don't even suffer too much; but it's maddening that she can't change. You'll be one of us, if she wants you to; besides, she's already started . . ."

Recognizing his own thoughts, Mariolle exclaimed, "Oh, I'm just the next in line, and I suspect she's not indifferent to titles."

"Not indifferent! But she laughs at them too. The most famous man in Paris, even the most distinguished, won't be there often if she doesn't take to him; yet she's fond of that idiot Fresnel, and that slimy Maltry. She clings to those fools for some reason, perhaps because they amuse her more than we do, perhaps because they really care for her more than we do—women like that more than anything else." And Lamarthe went on talking about her, arguing, analyzing, contradicting himself, questioned by Mariolle, replying with sincere feeling, fascinated by the subject and a little confused as well, his mind full of accurate observations and false deductions. "She's not the only one, you know: there are fifty women like her today, maybe more. For instance, that little Frémines who came in just a minute ago—she's another of the same kind only bolder, and married to a peculiar gent who makes his house an asylum for the most interesting lunatics in Paris. I drop in there quite often."

Without noticing where they were going, they had followed the boulevard Malesherbes to the rue Royale, then taken the Champs-Élysées all the way to the Arc de Triomphe, when Lamarthe suddenly looked at his watch. "My dear fellow, we've been talking about her for an hour and ten minutes—quite enough for today. I'll walk you to your club another time. Go home and go to bed. I'll do the same."

2

THE BIG room was full of daylight, its windows, walls, and ceiling draped with splendid chintz brought back from the East by an embassy friend; the yellow background made the cloth look as if it had been dipped in heavy cream, and the many-colored designs, mostly a brilliant Persian green, represented fanciful buildings with curved roofs, around which frisked periwigged lions, huge-horned antelopes, and brilliant birds-of-paradise.

There were few pieces of furniture. Three long tables, their green marble tops covered with whatever could assist in a woman's toilette. On the center table, large trays of heavy crystal; the one on the right offered an army of flagons, jars, and bottles of many sizes, all sealed with monogrammed silver stoppers. On the left-hand table were spread the countless tools and instruments of modern coquetry, so mysterious and delicate in their functions. In this whole room there were no more than two chaise longues and several low chairs, luxuriantly upholstered to receive a naked body, a languid limb. Then, occupying an entire wall, a huge space opened like a bright horizon; it consisted of three panels whose two lateral surfaces, on jointed hinges, allowed the young woman to see herself simultaneously in full face, in profile, and from behind, to enclose herself within her own image. To the right, in a niche usually curtained off, the tub, actually a deep basin, also of green marble, to which two steps led down. A bronze cupid—an elegant statuette by Prédolé—poured hot and cold water from the shells he was playing with. Deep in this alcove, a Venetian pier glass with many slanting panes rose up into a rounded vault, sheltering, enclosing, and reflecting, in each of its planes, the bath and the bather.

Just beyond, the writing desk, a simple piece of modern English design, covered with piles of letters, tiny torn-open envelopes, and loose sheets of paper glistening with gilded initials. For it was here that she wrote, and indeed here that she lived when she was alone.

Reclining on her chaise longue in a Chinese-silk dressing gown, her bare, firm arms revealed by the loose folds of the fabric, her hair pulled back and hanging behind her head in a twisted blond mass, Madame de Burne was daydreaming after her bath.

The maid knocked and entered, holding a letter which her mistress took from her, glanced at the handwriting, tore it open, and read the first lines, then murmured to her servant, "I'll ring for you in an hour."

Alone now, she relaxed into a smile of victory. The first words sufficed to indicate that here, at last, was Mariolle's declaration. He had resisted much longer than she might have predicted, for during the last three months she had deployed a greater array of attentions, a more elaborate expenditure of charm than she had ever produced for any of the *others*. He had seemed suspicious, forewarned, on guard against the ever-offered lure of her insatiable coquetry. It had taken many intimate conversations, during which she had mustered all the physical seduction of her person and the whole captivating effect of her wit, as well as many musical evenings during which, at the still-vibrating piano, sight-reading pages of scores filled with the souls of the masters, they had quivered with the same emotions, before she finally perceived in his eyes the avowal of a conquered soul, the imploring supplication of a yielding tenderness. How well she knew the signs! How often had she inspired, with feline skill and inextinguishable curiosity, that secret torment in the eyes of so many men! How it delighted her to feel them gradually subdued, vanquished, dominated by her invincible powers, as she became the Unique Idol, capricious and sovereign! These aptitudes had burgeoned within her quite gradually, gently, like a hidden instinct which subtly discloses itself, the instinct of war and conquest. During her years of marriage, a longing for revenge may have germinated within her heart, an obscure need to pay all men back for what she had received from one of them, to be the stronger in her turn, to bend their wills, to search out their resistances, and to make them suffer too.

But above all she was a born coquette, and once liberated, she set about pursuing and capturing her adorers as a hunter pursues game, for the simple pleasure of bringing it down. Yet her heart did not thirst for emotions like the hearts of sentimental women; she was not searching for a man's unique love nor for the gratification of a passion. All she required was the admiration of every man she met, the acknowledgment of capitulation, the homage of universal tenderness. Those who became the habitués of her house must also be the slaves of her beauty, and no intellectual interest could attach her for long to those who resisted her coquetries, disdainful of love's obligations or perhaps committed elsewhere. She required to be loved if she was to remain your friend, whereupon she offered unimaginable favors, delicious attentions, infinite vigilance to keep close to her those whom she had captivated. Once enrolled in her troop of admirers, it seemed that such men belonged to her by right of conquest. She ruled them all with a knowing skill, according to their defects and their qualities and the nature of their jealousy. Those who asked too much she expelled at the last possible moment, and when they sought readmission, having regained a certain discretion, she would impose severe conditions: she delighted in such perverse oscillations, finding as much pleasure in bewitching an elderly gentlemen as in turning the head of a smitten stripling.

Indeed she seemed to measure her own affection by the degree of ardor she had inspired; and fat Fresnel, dullest of companions, remained one of her favorites thanks to the frenzied passion by which he was so evidently possessed.

Not that she was utterly indifferent to the qualities of "her" men; how often she had privately entertained the initial stages of a feeling checked only at the moment it might have become dangerous. Each aspirant to her favors contributed a new note, and the unknown quality of each man's nature—particularly the artists, from whom she anticipated certain refinements, delicacies of emotion more intense and more original than the rest—had occasionally troubled her, awakening the intermittent dream of grand passions and enduring liaisons. But a prey to cautious fears, undecided and suspicious, she had always protected herself until the moment when the latest lover had ceased to move her. Then, too, she possessed the skeptical eyes of a modern woman which stripped the greatest men of their prestige in a few weeks. Once they were in love with her and had abandoned, in heartfelt confusion, their model poses and their paraded charms, she saw that like all their predecessors, they were no more than poor wretches whom she had subjugated by her seductive powers.

After all, for such a woman, of such evident talents, indeed of such perfections, to unite herself with any particular man, he would have to possess a great range of inestimable virtues!

And yet she was bored. How little she really enjoyed the society in which she had a secure position, enduring long evenings with stifled yawns and heavy eyelids, barely entertained by the aggressive whims, the shifting vogues for certain objects and certain beings, attached just enough not to be too easily disgusted by what she had so lately enjoyed or admired, and not enough to find authentic pleasure in any affection or interest, tormented by her nerves and not by her desires. Deprived of the absorbing preoccupations of simpler or more ardent souls, she lived in a kind of lambent tedium, without a shared faith in happiness, endlessly pursuing mere distractions and already burdened by lassitude, though she considered herself satisfied with the life she was privileged to lead.

Satisfied because she was convinced she must be the most seductive and the most sought after of women. Proud of her charm, whose power she had tested so often, well pleased by her somewhat irregular and captivating beauty, confident of the acuteness of her mind by which she intuited and understood so many things that others quite failed to see, reveling in her wit which so many gifted men appreciated, and unaware of the limitations of her intellect and education, she considered herself a creature virtually unique, a singular pearl cast in a mediocre world which struck her as somewhat barren and monotonous precisely because she was too good for it.

Never would she have suspected herself to be the unconscious cause of the continuous boredom she suffered from; she blamed others for it and held them responsible for her melancholy. If they could not manage to divert her sufficiently, to amuse and even to attract her, it was because they lacked talents, charm, authentic qualities. "Everyone," she would say with a laugh, "everyone's so boring. The only bearable ones are the people I like, and only because I like them."

And the best way to give her pleasure was to find her incomparable. Quite aware that there would be no success without *some* venture, she put all her efforts into seduction and found nothing more agreeable than savoring the homage of a melting glance, a choked word, fresh tribute from the heart, that violent muscle a word could set pounding.

Consequently she had been quite surprised by her difficulty in making a conquest of André Mariolle, for from the first day she was aware that he had been delighted by her. Then, of course, she had divined his skittish nature, secretly envious and subtly egotistical, and to overcome his resistances she had lavished upon him so many considerations, so many preferences, and so much natural sympathy that he had ultimately surrendered.

This last month, certainly, she had realized that he was captured, uneasy in her presence now, taciturn and feverish, yet resisting avowal. Oh, those avowals! Actually she didn't enjoy them much, for if they were too direct, too expressive, she knew she would have to cut them short. Once or twice, when they became too intense, she was obliged to lose her temper and close her door. What she liked best were delicate insinuations, half confidences, discreet allusions, moral genuflections, and to obtain such expressive reserve from her admirers she exercised exceptional tact and skill.

For a month now she had been expecting and looking forward to a phrase from Mariolle's lips, veiled or explicit, according to his nature, by which his oppressed heart might find relief.

He said nothing, but he had written—a long letter: four pages! She held it in her hands, trembling with satisfaction. She stretched out on her chaise longue to be more comfortable and let her slippers drop to the carpet as she read. She was surprised by what she found. He was telling her, quite seriously, that he refused to suffer at her hands, that he already knew her too well to consent to be another of her victims. In very polite phrases, loaded with compliments and in which his repressed love was quite evident, he left her in no doubt that he knew how she dealt with men, that he too was caught in her toils but that he would free himself from this servitude by leaving before it began. He had only to recommence his old wandering life. He was going away.

The letter was a farewell, an eloquent and determined farewell!

Of course she was astonished as she read and reread these four pages of tenderly irritated and impassioned prose. She stood, put on her slippers, and began pacing up and down, her hands partly thrust into her dressing gown's tiny pockets, holding in one the crumpled letter.

Shocked by this unexpected declaration, the first thing she thought was: "How well the boy writes—better than Lamarthe! He's quite touching, and not even striving for effect."

She went over to the table with the silver-crested flagons and took a cigarette out of a Dresden box; having lit it, she walked toward the mirror where she saw three young women approaching her in the three hinged panels. When she was quite close she stopped short, made a slight bow, smiled, and nodded as if to say, "Pretty—very pretty!" She inspected her eyes, showed her teeth, raised her arms, set her hands on her hips, turned to see all of herself in the three mirrors, tilting her head slightly.

Then she remained standing in front of herself, enveloped by the triple reflection of her body which she found so charming, delighted by what she saw and taking a physical satisfaction in her beauty, savoring it with a sort of tenderness almost as sensual as that of a man.

She was quite accustomed to such scrutiny on a daily basis; and her maid, who had often surprised her at the glass, once teased her by saying, "Madame will wear out every mirror in the house."

Yet this self-satisfaction was the secret of her charm and of her power over men. By dint of admiring herself, of cherishing the subtleties of her expression and the elegance of her figure, and of cultivating whatever could enhance them, discovering imperceptible nuances which made her loveliness more powerful in less accustomed eyes, by pursuing every artifice that might increase her grace, she had naturally discovered everything which might please others most.

Had she been more beautiful, and more indifferent to her beauty, she would have lacked the seduction which enchanted anyone not entirely rebellious to the nature of her power.

A little weary of standing motionless so long, she spoke to her still-smiling image (and her image, in the triple mirrors, moved its lips to repeat): "We'll see about that, monsieur." Then crossing the room, she sat down at her desk and wrote:

Dear Monsieur Mariolle,
   Come and see me tomorrow at four. I shall be alone, and I hope to reassure you as to the imaginary dangers you fear. I call myself your friend, and shall prove to you I am one.
                                        Michèle de Burne

How simply she dressed to receive André Mariolle's visit the next afternoon! A little gray dress with a tinge of lilac, melancholy as twilight and quite plain, with a high collar and long sleeves, close-fitting at throat and waist and hips.

When he came in, looking rather serious, she walked toward him, holding out both hands. He kissed them, and they both sat down. She allowed the silence to last several moments, to make sure of his embarrassment. He evidently did not know what to say and was waiting for her to speak. At last she broke the silence. "Well now! Let's come to the point straight off. What's happening here? Do you realize that you've written me a very rude letter?"

"I know I have, and I apologize. I am—I've always been—much too frank, with everyone... I could have gone away without these uncalled-for and wounding explanations. But I thought —I believed it would be more *loyal* if I behaved according to my nature and trusted to your understanding—"

She broke in, speaking in a tone of pitying contentment. "Now, now! What kind of silliness is that?"

Impetuously, he exclaimed, "I'd prefer not to speak of it—"

And she broke in again, without letting him continue. "I've asked you here in order to speak of it; and we *shall* speak of it, until you're quite convinced you're in no danger." Then she giggled like a girl, and the touch of convent school in her gown made her merriment all the more natural.

He burst out with the words: "What I wrote you is the truth, the simple truth I'm afraid of."

Serious again, she answered, "All right. I know that. It happens to all my friends. You also wrote me that I am a dreadful coquette: I admit it—but no one's ever died of it; I don't even think anyone's ever suffered from it. This must be what Lamarthe calls the crisis. You're going through it now, it passes, and then comes—what?—a sort of chronic condition which doesn't hurt anyone and which I keep over a low flame for all my friends, so that they remain devoted to me, attached to me, faithful to me. Isn't that it? You see, I'm sincere too, as frank as you are, monsieur. Do you know many women who would dare tell a man what I've just told you?"

Her expression was so comical and yet so determined, so

simple and yet so provocative, that he couldn't keep from smiling in his turn.

"All your friends," he said, "are men who have often passed through that fire, even before meeting you. Already seared and grilled, they can take the heat you have in store for them. But I, madame—I've never been through that fire. And I've felt for some time that it would be a terrible thing if I surrendered to the feeling now growing in my heart."

She grew suddenly familiar, and leaning toward him, her hands crossed on her knees, spoke in a low, decisive tone. "Listen to me: I'm speaking in good faith. I'd hate to lose a friend on account of a fear I consider a chimera. You'll love me, granted! But men today don't love women to the point of really doing themselves any harm. Believe me, I know both sides of the matter." She remained silent a moment, then added with the odd smile of a woman telling the truth but believing she's lying: "Besides, I don't have what's required to be madly adored. I'm too modern for that. Look, I'll be a friend, a lovely friend for whom you feel some real affection, but no more than that—I'll see to it." And she added, more seriously: "In any case, I warn you that I'm quite incapable of really loving anyone—I'll treat you like the others, no better and no worse. I have a horror of tyrannies—of tyrants. I had to put up with all that from a husband; but from a friend, from a real friend, I don't care to accept those despotisms of affection which are the ruin of cordial relations. You see, I'm hiding nothing from you—I'm speaking to you as a friend. Won't you agree to accept the role of 'loyal friend' I'm offering you? If not, it's not too late to go away, whatever the seriousness of your case. 'A lover gone, a lover cured,' you know…"

He looked at her, already won over by her voice, her gestures, the entire intoxication of her person, and he murmured, quite resigned and enthralled by feeling her so close to him, "Madame, I accept your offer, and if suffering comes of it, so much the worse for me. You're quite worth suffering for."

She stopped him. "Now we won't say anything more about it,"

she said. "We won't ever speak of it again." And she began talking about things that didn't trouble him in the slightest. An hour later he left, in torment because he loved her, and happy because she had asked him not to go away and he had promised he would not.

3

He was in torment because he loved her. Unlike vulgar lovers whose heart's choice is aureoled by perfections, he had fallen in love with a woman perceived by the clear-sighted vision of a suspicious and defiant man who has never been entirely captured. His restless mind, penetrating and indolent, ever on the defensive, had hitherto preserved him from passion. A few affairs, two brief liaisons slain by boredom, and several expensive ventures broken off by disgust—nothing more, in the entire history of his soul. He regarded women as objects of utility for those who wanted children and a well-kept household, as objects of relative pleasure for those in search of love's pastimes.

Before coming to Madame de Burne's house, he had been warned against her by all his friends. What he knew about her interested him, intrigued him, pleased him, yet rather repelled him. In principle, he disliked players who never pay up. After the first encounters, he had found her extremely amusing and animated with a special and contagious charm; the natural and cultivated beauty of this shapely, delicate blond person who seemed at once svelte and plump, with splendid arms that were made for embraces, with what he guessed to be long slender legs made for flight, like a gazelle's, with feet so small and so light that they left no traces, impressed him as a sort of symbol of all his vain hopes. Further, in his exchanges with her, he found a pleasure he had thought impossible in mere salon conversation. For all her teasing irony, there were moments when she let herself be overcome by sentimental and intellectual influences, as if, beneath her gaiety, there lingered the age-old shadow of the poetic tenderness of an earlier age. It was a touch of inconsistency which rendered her captivating.

She made much of Mariolle, eager to conquer him as she had the others; and he came to her house as often as he could, drawn by a growing need to see her more and more frequently. There was power emanating from her which overcame him, a power of charm, of attention, of smiles and speech, irresistible though he often left feeling irritated by something she had said or done.

The more he felt this inexpressible fluid entering his very being, making him subservient to her, the more he understood her, realized what she was, and suffered from her nature, ardently wishing she were different.

Yet the very characteristics he disliked in her were just what had seduced and conquered him in spite of himself, for all his consciousness of them—more so, perhaps, than her better qualities.

Her coquetry, which she displayed quite openly, like a fan she would spread or close in front of everyone, depending on which men attracted and addressed her; her way of taking nothing seriously, which on those first occasions he found so diverting but now seemed so sinister; her constant need of distraction, of novelty, insatiably growing in her ever-wearied heart, all this occasionally left him so exasperated that he resolved, on returning home, to lessen his frequent visits and eventually discontinue them altogether.

The next day, he would find some excuse to return. What he found becoming more intense, as he fell deeper in love, was the insecurity of his feelings and the certainty of suffering. No, he wasn't blind; he was gradually sinking into this sentiment like a man drowning from exhaustion because his boat has capsized and he is too far from shore. He knew her as well as she could be known, the prescience of passion having sharpened his insight, and he could no longer keep from thinking about her at every moment. With tireless persistence, he still sought to analyze, to illuminate the darkness of this female soul, an incomprehensible mixture of giddy intelligence and disenchantment, of reason and childishness, of affectionate appearance and fickleness, all those contradictory inclinations united to form so seductive and bewildering a creature.

Yet how had she managed to gain this mastery over him? He kept asking himself this question over and over, and failing to answer it, for a reflective, observant, and proudly modest nature like his ought logically to have looked for traditionally peaceful qualities, the tender charm and constant attachment which would assure a man's happiness. But in this woman he had come up against something unexpected, a sort of departure from the human race, exciting by its very novelty—a creature who inaugurated a new generation, like nothing ever seen before, and who spreads around herself, even by her imperfections, the dangerous glow of an awakening.

After the passionate and whimsical dreamers of the Restoration had come the joyous daughters of the empire, convinced of the reality of pleasure; whereupon had appeared this new transformation of the Ewig-Weibliche, a refined creature of wandering sensibility, an agitated, anxious, irresolute spirit which seemed to have already tested every drug to lull and rouse the nerves, the chloroform which subjugates, as well as the ether and morphine which lash the imagination, lull the senses, and eliminate the emotions.

In her he enjoyed the savor of a factitious creature, created and cultivated to charm—an object of rare luxury, alluring, exquisite, and delicate, to whom all eyes turned, before whom hearts beat faster and desires sharpened, as the appetite is excited in the presence of fine victuals behind a pane of glass, prepared and displayed to rouse hunger.

Once he realized he was sliding down the slopes of an abyss, he began to reflect with alarm upon the dangers of his fall. What would become of him? What would she do? Doubtless what she had done with all the others: she would bring him to that condition in which a man follows a woman's whims like a dog his master's footsteps, and he would be installed in her collection of more or less illustrious favorites. But had she actually played this game with all the others? Hadn't there been one man, just one, whom she had loved, truly loved, for a month, a day, a hour, with one of those swiftly checked impulses which had now overcome his own heart?

He discussed her interminably with the others, leaving the dinners where they had all come to warm their hearts in her presence. He realized they were still troubled, discontent, anxious, men whom no reality has satisfied.

No, she had loved no one among these salon celebrities; but he, who was no one beside them, who attracted no notice when his name was announced in a gathering, what would he be for her? Nothing, no one, a walk-on whose intimacy is taken for granted, as convenient and flavorless as watered wine.

Had he been a famous man, he would have accepted such a role: his celebrity would have made it less humiliating. As a nonentity, he could not endure it. And he wrote her to say farewell.

When he had received her brief reply, he was moved by it as though a great benison had fallen to his lot, and when she had extracted his promise not to go away, he was overjoyed, as by a deliverance from some great danger.

Several days passed without anything occurring between them; but when the lull that follows a storm was over, he felt the embers of his desire burning once more, more intensely than ever. He had resolved never again to speak of it to her, but he had not promised not to write; and late one night, when he suffered in the restless vigils of love's insomnia, he sat down at his desk, almost in spite of himself, and began to set down his feelings on paper. It was nothing like a letter, merely notes, phrases, fragments of suffering which turned into words.

This soothed him; he had relieved his anguish somewhat, and stretching out on his bed, he could fall asleep at last.

On waking the next morning, he reread the pages, finding a tremulous life in them, thrust them in an envelope, wrote her address on it, kept the thing until that night, then posted it so that it would reach her when she awoke the next morning.

He assured himself that she would not take offense at these few sheets of paper. The shiest of women regard a sincere love letter with infinite indulgence. And such letters, written by trembling hands on tear-stained paper, surely have an invincible power over any and all hearts.

Late in the day, he went to her house, to learn how she would receive him and what she might say. He found Monsieur de Pradon chatting with his daughter, smoking one cigarette after another; he would often spend time with her in this way, for he seemed to treat her less as a daughter than as a friend. She had imparted to their relationship, and to their affection for each other, a touch of the loving homage she paid to herself and demanded of everyone else.

When she saw Mariolle come in, her face brightened with pleasure. She was quick to hold out her hand, smiling as if to say, "I'm so glad to see you."

Mariolle hoped that the father would soon withdraw, but Monsieur de Pradon had no such intention. Though he knew his daughter and harbored no suspicions of her behavior with men, he liked to surround her with an inquisitive, slightly anxious, almost marital attention. Besides, he was curious to learn what chances of lasting success this new friend might have: Would he be a passing fancy, like so many others, or a member of the regular circle?

So Monsieur de Pradon made himself comfortable, and Mariolle realized at once that he was not to be dislodged. He decided to play the older man's game and indeed to win him over if he could, supposing that favor from this quarter, or at least neutrality, would be worth more than hostility. He made every effort to be lively and even gay, with no trace of the suitor in his manner. Madame de Burne was pleased with this behavior: "He's a bright boy who knows how to plays his part." And Monsieur de Pradon was thinking: "Now here's an agreeable fellow whose head my daughter hasn't turned, not like all the other fools."

When Mariolle decided the moment had come to take his leave, both father and daughter had been thoroughly charmed. But he left the house with a troubled mind. In this woman's company, he was already suffering from the captivity in which she held him, feeling that he would seek admission to this heart in vain—like a jailed man pounding on an iron door.

A prisoner!—he was sure of it now, and no longer attempted to free himself from his bonds; and since he was unable to escape his fate, he resolved to be cunning, patient, stubborn, to win her by skill, by the homage for which she was so greedy, by the adoration which intoxicated her, by the voluntary servitude to which he would allow himself to be reduced.

His letter had pleased her. He would write. And he wrote. Almost every night, coming home, at the moment when the mind, inflamed by the day's agitations, sees its concerns and its designs enlarged like a hallucination, he would sit at his desk under the lamp, take a deep breath, and think of her. The seed of poetry, which so many men, in their soul's sloth, allow to die, germinated in this impulse. By writing the same things, the same *thing*, his love, in forms which the daily renewal of his desire revived, he kindled his ardor by this task of literary devotion. He sought by day and discovered by night those irresistible expressions which overexcited emotion draws from the brain like so many sparks. Blowing thus on the embers in his heart, he ignited them, for truly passionate love letters are often more dangerous for the writer than for their recipient.

By keeping himself in this state of effervescence, heating his blood with words and dressing his soul in a single thought, he gradually lost any notion of this woman's reality. Ceasing to judge her as she had initially appeared to him, he no longer perceived her now save through the lyricism of his own phrases, and everything he wrote to her each night became in his heart no more than so many truths. This daily labor of idealization showed her to him more or less as he would have seen her in his dreams. His former resistances fell, moreover, before the undeniable affection Madame de Burne showed him. Of course, though they said nothing to each other on these occasions, she preferred him to all others and openly showed as much. And so he came to believe, with a kind of insane hope, that she might end by loving him.

She yielded, in fact, with a complex and naïve delight, to the spell of those letters. No one had ever adored her, ever cherished her in this fashion, with this kind of silent reserve. No one had ever conceived the charming notion of sending to her bedside, when she awakened each morning, on the little silver tray which the maid offered her, this breakfast of sentiment in a paper envelope. And most precious of all to her was the fact that he himself never alluded to the circumstance, as if he knew nothing of it and remained, in her salon, the coolest of her friends, never referring to that torrent of affection with which he covered her in secret.

Of course she had received love letters, but in another tonality, less reserved, more urgent, letters that were more like demands. For three months, his three months of *crisis*, Lamarthe had devoted a charming correspondence to her, the pages of a spellbound novelist who made feelings his literary stock in trade. She kept in her desk, in a secret drawer, these delicate and alluring epistles from a deeply stirred writer who had caressed her with his pen up to the day he lost all hope of success.

Mariolle's letters were quite different: their concentration of desire so energetic, their sincerity of expression so just, their submission so complete, and their devotion promising to be so lasting, that she received them, opened them, and devoured them with a pleasure no writing had ever afforded her.

Her friendship for the man showed as much, and she invited him to come to see her even more often, since he brought to their relationship such absolute discretion and seemed to be unaware, in speaking to her, that he had ever used a sheet of paper on which to express his adoration. Moreover she judged the situation to be quite original, worthy of a book, and found, in her profound satisfaction, that here beside her was a man who loved her in this way, a sort of active leaven of sympathy which made her consider him a being apart.

Hitherto, in all the hearts she had troubled, she had detected, despite the vanity of her coquetry, certain alien absorptions: she did not reign there alone; instead she discerned powerful preoccupations which had nothing to do with her. Jealous of music with Massival, of literature with Lamarthe, inevitably of *something*; dissatisfied with her half successes, powerless to clear the field of a rival in these souls of ambitious men, of famous men, of artists for whom vocation is a mistress from whom nothing and no one can sever them, she had now, for the first time, encountered a man for whom she was all and everything. Or so at least he swore. Only fat Fresnel loved her as much, to be sure. But he was fat Fresnel. She surmised that no one had ever been possessed by her in this fashion; and her selfish gratitude to the young man who afforded her this triumph assumed the qualities of tenderness. She needed him now, needed his presence, needed his regard, needed his servitude, that domesticity of love. If he flattered her vanity less than others, he flattered more those sovereign requirements which govern any coquette's body and soul: her pride and her instinct of domination, that fierce instinct of female peace.

Like an invaded country, she took gradual possession of his life by a series of tiny encroachments, more numerous day by day. She organized parties, expeditions to the theater, dinners in restaurants in order to be certain of his company; she led him in her train with a conqueror's satisfaction; she could no longer do without him, or rather without the slavery to which he had been reduced.

And he followed her, happy to be made so much of, fondled by her eyes, her voice, her every whim; and lived now in a continuous transport of desire, of a love as burning and bewildering as a high fever.

PART TWO

I

MARIOLLE had just arrived at her house. He would wait for her, since she had not yet arrived, though that morning she had sent him a *petit bleu* to meet her there.

In this salon, where he had spent so many delighted hours, where everything pleased him, he nonetheless felt, each time he was alone in the room, an oppression of the heart, a kind of breathlessness, an anxiety, which kept him from remaining in his chair as long as she had not appeared. He paced up and down in happy expectation, with the fear that some obstacle might have kept her from returning, which would put off their meeting till the next day.

When he heard a carriage draw up in front of the street door, he had a shiver of hope, and when the apartment bell rang, he doubted no longer. She came in, her hat still on her head, which was unusual for her, seeming both hurried and happy. "I have some news for you."

"And what would that be, madame?"

She met his eyes and burst out laughing. "It would be that I'm going away—to the country for a while."

At once he was filled with deep disappointment, and his face fell. "Why tell me a thing like that as if it were good news?"

"Just sit down, and I'll tell you all about it. You know, or maybe you don't, that Monsieur Valsaci, my poor mother's brother, a civil engineer who builds bridges, has a place near Avranches where he spends some of his time with his wife and children—that's where he has his practice. We always visit them every summer.

This year I didn't want to go, but he was annoyed and made a terrible fuss about it to Papa. By the way, I must tell you that Papa's very jealous of you and makes terrible scenes—he claims I'm compromising myself with you. You'll have to come less often. But don't worry, I'll fix things. Anyway, Papa scolded me and made me promise to spend ten days or maybe two weeks in Avranches. We're leaving Tuesday morning. What do you say to that?"

"I say that you're breaking my heart."

"Is that all?"

"Well, what do you want me to say? I can't keep you from going!"

"You can't think of anything?"

"No . . . Not that I . . . How should I know? What do you suggest?"

"Well, here's my idea. Avranches is quite near Mont-Saint-Michel. Do you know Mont-Saint-Michel?"

"No, madame."

"Well, next Friday, you'll be inspired with a desire to see that marvel. You'll put up at Avranches, you'll go for a stroll Saturday evening, for example, at sunset in the park overlooking the bay. We'll meet there quite by chance. Papa will frown, but I don't care. I'll organize an expedition for us all to visit the abbey the next day. Show some enthusiasm and be charming, the way you can when you want to. Make a conquest of my aunt and invite us all to dinner at the inn where you'll be staying. We'll stay there for the night, and we won't separate until the next day. You'll return by way of Saint-Malo, and eight days later I'll be back in Paris. Isn't that a splendid plan? Aren't I a nice person?"

He murmured in a burst of gratitude, "You're everything I love best in the world."

"Hush!"

And their eyes met for a few seconds. She smiled, and in that smile expressed her heartfelt sympathy, her gratitude, as tender as it was sincere. His eyes searched hers as if he could devour her where she sat. He wanted to fall at her feet, to bite the hem of her dress, to shout something, and most of all to make her see that he was at a loss to tell her what filled him from head to foot, body and soul, something inexpressibly grievous since he couldn't show it—his love, his delicious and terrible love.

But she understood him without his saying a word, the way a marksman realizes his bullet has hit the bull's-eye. She understood that she alone filled this man now, that he belonged to her more than she belonged to herself. And this made her happy, and she found him charming. She said, in a good-humored tone, "Then it's all arranged. We'll make this expedition."

His voice husky with emotion, he stammered, "Yes of course, madame, it's all arranged."

Then, after another silence, she resumed without further excuses. "I won't keep you any longer today. I came back just to tell you this, since we're leaving the day after tomorrow. I'll be busy all day tomorrow, and I still have four or five errands to run before dinner."

He stood up immediately; he was in torment, for his only desire was never to leave her; and having kissed her hands, took his leave with a heavy heart, yet filled with hope.

Then came four long days he had to get through somehow. He spent them in Paris, seeing no one, preferring silence to voices, solitude to friends. And on Friday morning he took the eight o'clock express, having hardly slept a wink in feverish anticipation of this journey. He had felt imprisoned in his dark bedroom where the only sounds that reached him came from passing late-night fiacres, suggesting longed-for departures.

As soon as the sickly light of early dawn appeared between the drawn curtains, he jumped out of bed, opened the window, and scanned the sky, haunted by fear of bad weather. The day promised to be fair. There was a faint mist in the air—it would be hot later on. He dressed much sooner than he needed to, ready two hours ahead of time, impatient to be out of the house and on his way at last. He sent his servant for a fiacre before he had even finished washing: What if he failed to find one?

The first jolts of the carriage were a presage of bliss, but when he made his way into the Gare Montparnasse, he was appalled to realize that he had fifty minutes to wait. Finding an empty compartment, he paid for every seat in order to be alone and to daydream undisturbed.

When he felt the express start up, gliding toward *her* with its swift, gentle motion, his eagerness was intensified instead of being relieved, and he suffered a child's stupid longing to press both his hands against the upholstered partition in order to accelerate the train's speed.

For the long hours until noon he was immured in his anticipations and paralyzed by his hopes; then little by little, once past Argentan, his eyes were drawn to the lush Norman countryside outside the window. The train was passing through a wide, rolling landscape, where the farms and orchards were bordered by huge trees whose rich foliage seemed to glisten in the sunshine. July was almost over, that vigorous season when every plant in this fertile land was burgeoning with sap and reaching its peak growth. In every pasture, linked and separated by high walls of leaves, huge blond oxen, cows mottled with strange patterns on their flanks, fierce auburn bulls with broad foreheads and curly chests stood at the stiles or low in the high grass, munching contentedly as the train rushed through the deep, fresh countryside, the very soil seeming to exude cider and beef.

Everywhere tiny streams glistened at the roots of poplars and beneath the pale veils of willows; rivulets flashed for a second in the grass, vanished to reappear farther on, bathing the whole scene in moist fertility. And for a while Mariolle allowed himself to be distracted from his love by the swift and continuous procession of splendid apple trees dotting a parkland inhabited by herds of cattle.

But once he had changed trains at Folligny, impatience to arrive seized him once again, and for the last forty minutes he must have pulled his watch out of its pocket twenty times. He leaned out of the window at every moment and finally glimpsed, on a high hill, the town where *she* was waiting for him. The train must have been late, and only an hour separated him from the moment when he would encounter her, by chance, on the public promenade.

He was the only traveler to board the hotel omnibus, its horses slowly climbing the steep road to Avranches, where the houses at the cliff top gave the place the look, from a distance, of a fortified citadel. Once inside the walls, the Norman stronghold turned out to be a charming old town, with tiny regular houses that seemed almost identical pressing against each other with a kind of ancient pride and modest comfort, both rustic and medieval.

Once Mariolle had dropped his suitcase in a room at the inn, he asked for directions to the botanical garden, and proceeded to make his way there immediately, though he was ahead of the appointed hour. He hoped that she too might have been early.

At the gate, a glance informed him that the place was empty, or virtually so. Three old men were strolling about, evidently shopkeepers who took this same exercise every afternoon. A family of English boys and girls with skinny legs were playing around a blond governess who seemed, in her distracted gaze, to be dreaming of something other than her charges.

His heart pounding, Mariolle walked straight ahead, staring down each path he crossed. He followed a broad allée of huge elms diagonally dividing the garden, their dense green foliage forming a lofty vault, and suddenly emerged onto a terrace from which the horizon dominated in all directions; he was utterly overwhelmed by the sight that met his eyes. At the foot of the hill extended an interminable plain of sand that melted into a distant sea. Across it meandered a river, and beneath the brilliant blue sky sun-flecked pools seemed to form patches of another sky underground.

In the center of this yellow desert, still steeped in the receding tide, rose up, ten or twelve kilometers offshore, a fantastic pyramidal crag with a cathedral at its summit. Amid these huge dunes, Tombelaine—a single neighboring reef squatting amid its quicksands—reared its round back above the tides. Farther on, in the bluish stripe of the sea, other sunken crags showed their brown crests; and alongside this sandy waste but farther to the right extended vast green stretches of the Norman countryside, so thick with trees it seemed a single limitless forest. Here all nature seemed to reveal itself at once, in its grandeur and its grace, and Mariolle's gaze wandered from this vision of forests to that nearer apparition of the granite mount that was the coast's sole inhabit-ant, its strange Gothic silhouette rising out of the measureless sands.

Mariolle had frequently experienced the peculiar pleasure a traveler receives from contact with unknown terrain, but this time the shock was so sudden that he stood perfectly still, astonished and delighted, forgetting his pinioned heart. But the sound of church bells made him turn around, suddenly reminded of his eagerness for their meeting. The garden was still almost empty. The English children had vanished, and only the three old men were still making their monotonous rounds. He began to imitate them.

She would come any minute now. He would see her at the end of one of the paths leading to this wonderful terrace. He would recognize her figure, her gait, then her face and her smile, and he would hear her voice. What happiness! What happiness! He felt that she was near, somewhere, not to be found or seen yet, but thinking of him, she too knowing she would soon be seeing him again.

He nearly uttered a cry: a blue parasol, just the dome of a para-sol was gliding down below him, around a flower bed. It was *she*, without a doubt. A little boy appeared, rolling a hoop; then two ladies—he recognized *her*—then two men: her father and an-other gentleman. She was all in blue, like a spring sky. Oh yes, he recognized her without even making out her features, but dared not move toward her, knowing he would stammer and blush, un-able to explain this accidental meeting under Monsieur de Pra-don's suspicious gaze.

But he walked toward them nonetheless, his field glasses pressed to his eyes, apparently absorbed in studying the horizon. It was she who called out his name, without even bothering to seem surprised. "Hello, Monsieur Mariolle. Wonderful view, isn't it?"

Startled by this greeting, he wasn't sure how to reply, and stammered, "Ah, it's you madame, what luck to meet you here! I was just exploring this wonderful countryside——"

She broke in with a smile: "And you chose the very moment I was here. How very kind of you." And she made the introductions. "One of my best friends, Monsieur Mariolle; my aunt, Madame Valsaci, my uncle, who builds bridges." After the ritual greetings, Monsieur de Pradon and the young man from Paris exchanged a chilly handshake, and the promenade continued. She had put him between herself and her aunt, after giving him a quick glance, one of those glances that seem to be a challenge, and then continued: "What do you think of this part of the world?"

"I've rarely seen anything more beautiful."

"Oh, if you'd been here as long as I have, you'd find it really gets inside you. It has a tremendous effect. The sea coming and going over the sand, that ceaseless movement, covering everything twice a day, and so quickly—a galloping horse couldn't escape it—and this wonderful spectacle of the sky, free to us all: I find it all so moving, I'm quite carried away—wasn't I just telling you that, Aunt Marie?"

Madame Valsaci, an elderly gray-haired woman with an air of provincial distinction, the respected spouse of a prominent civil engineer incapable of setting aside his professional stiffness, acknowledged she had never seen her niece in such a state of enthusiasm. And then she added, as if upon reflection: "It's not surprising though, when one remembers that she's scarcely seen or admired any scenery except at the theater."

"Oh Aunt, I go to Dieppe and Trouville almost every year."

The old lady laughed. "People go to Dieppe and Trouville to meet their friends. The sea is only there to allow bathers to arrange a rendezvous." This was spoken quite simply, perhaps without any special meaning.

They were back at the terrace, which irresistibly attracted them—people came in spite of themselves, from every point in the garden, like balls rolling down a slope. The declining sun seemed to spread a sheet of transparent gold behind the mount's high silhouette, which darkened as they walked, like a huge reliquary under a shimmering veil. But Mariolle had eyes only for the beloved blond figure walking beside him, wrapped in a blue cloud. Never had she seemed so delicious. She was changed without his knowing exactly how—there was an inexplicable freshness in her flesh, her eyes, her hair, and somehow in her soul, a freshness that echoed this landscape, this sky, this light, this foliage. He had never known her like this, never loved her so much.

He walked beside her now without finding a word to say; and the rustle of her gown, the occasional touch of her elbow, the eloquent meeting of their eyes utterly annihilated him, as if they had canceled his personality as a man. He felt he had suddenly been destroyed by this woman's contact, absorbed by her to the point of being nothing now but a desire, an appeal, nothing but an adoration. She had suppressed his entire past existence, the way a letter is consumed in the fire.

She saw it too, she realized how absolute her victory was, and she was touched and somehow excited, feeling even more alive in this country air that was also the air of the sea, so full of sun and sap, and she said, without looking at him, "I'm so happy to see you!" And she quickly added: "How much time do you have left here?"

"Two days," he answered, "if today counts for one." Then, turning to her aunt: "Would Madame Valsaci do me the honor of spending the day, tomorrow, at Mont-Saint-Michel with her husband?"

Madame de Burne answered for her aunt. "I won't let her refuse, since we've been lucky enough to run into you here."

To which the civil engineer's wife added: "Yes, of course, monsieur, we accept with pleasure, provided you'll dine with us tonight."

He bowed his acceptance. And suddenly he was filled with a kind of delirious joy, the joy that overwhelms you on receiving news of what you long for most. What had he achieved? What new development had suddenly occurred? Nothing. All the same he was elated, stirred by an indefinable premonition.

They walked a good while along the terrace, waiting for the sun to set in order to see, at the very last minute, the mount's jagged black shadow incised on the fiery horizon. And they talked of the simplest things, repeating whatever can be said in front of a stranger and occasionally glancing at each other.

Then they made their way to the villa, built on the outskirts of Avranches, in the center of a splendid garden overlooking the bay.

Determined to be discreet, and a little worried, moreover, by Monsieur de Pradon's cold and almost hostile attitude, Mariolle left the party quite early. When he held Madame de Burne's fingers to his lips, she said to him twice, with a peculiar intonation, "Till tomorrow... till tomorrow."

As soon as he had gone, Monsieur and Madame Valsaci, who were used to keeping early hours, proposed retiring for the night.

"You go," said Madame de Burne, "I'll take a turn around the garden."

And her father added: "So will I." She left the house, wrapping a shawl around her shoulders, and they began walking side by side along the white gravel paths which the full moon picked out like tiny winding streams among the lawns and flower beds. "My dear child, you will do me the justice to grant that I've never given you advice?"

She guessed what was coming and readied herself for the attack. "I beg your pardon, Papa, but at least once you gave me a piece of advice."

"I did?"

"Yes, you certainly did."

"Something concerning your... your life?"

"Yes, and very bad advice it was. So I'm quite determined, if you have more advice to give me now, not to take it."

"What advice did I give you?"

"You advised me to marry Monsieur de Burne, which proves you lack judgment, perception, and knowledge of human beings in general and of your daughter in particular."

He was silent for a moment, a little surprised and embarrassed, and then, very slowly, resumed. "Yes, I made a mistake that time. But I am confident I'm not mistaken about the fatherly advice it's my duty to give you today."

"Say what it is, in any case. I'll do what I must."

"You're on the verge of compromising yourself." She burst out laughing, a little too quickly, and completed his thought. "With Monsieur Mariolle, no doubt?"

"With Monsieur Mariolle."

"You're forgetting, Papa, that I've compromised myself already with Monsieur Georges de Maltry, with Monsieur Massival, with Monsieur Gaston de Lamarthe, with a dozen other gentlemen of whom you were similarly jealous, for I cannot find a single nice, devoted man without my entire acquaintance exploding in rage, you first of all, you whom nature has bestowed upon me as a Noble Father and a director-general of my—"

"No, no, you've never compromised yourself with anyone. You always behave, in your relations with your friends, with the utmost tact."

She answered sharply, "Papa dear, I'm no longer a little girl, and I promise not to compromise myself with Monsieur Mariolle any more than with the others. Have no fear. However, I admit that it was I who asked him to come here. I find him delightful— as intelligent as all his predecessors and much less self-centered. Which was also your opinion, until the day you thought you had discovered that I somewhat...preferred him. Oh, you're not so sly as all that! I know you pretty well, Papa, and I could tell you a thing or two, if I wanted to. So since Monsieur Mariolle pleases me, I decided that it would be extremely pleasant *accidentally* to arrange a nice little excursion, and that it is stupid to deprive oneself of anything that might be amusing when one is in no danger. And I am certainly in no danger of compromising myself, since you are here, Papa." And she laughed again, quite naturally this time, certain that her every word was telling, that she had trapped him in the acknowledgment of a rather suspect jealousy she had perceived long since, and could now entertain herself with her discovery by indulging in an inadmissible and bold coquetry.

Monsieur de Pradon said nothing, irritated and embarrassed, feeling too that she had divined, deep in his fatherly solicitude, a mysterious rancor whose origin he had no desire to clarify. And she added: "You have nothing to fear. It is quite natural at this season to make an excursion to Mont-Saint-Michel with my aunt and uncle, with you, Father, and with a friend. Besides, no one will know anything about it. And if anything were to be known, no one could say a word. Once back in Paris, I shall see to it that this friend returns to his place with the rest."

"So be it," he sighed. "Let it be as if I had not spoken."

They walked on a little, and Monsieur de Pradon asked, "Shall we go back to the house? I'm tired and I'm going to bed."

"No, I'll stay out a little longer. It's such a lovely night."

He murmured, with evident meaning, "Don't go far. You never know whom you might run into."

"Oh, I'll stay right under your window."

"All right then, good night, my dear child." He kissed her quickly on the forehead, and went indoors.

She walked on a ways and sat down on a little rustic bench beneath an oak. The night was warm and filled with the breath of the fields and a brownish mist from the sea, for under the full moon the bay was swathed in vapors that crept like white smoke across the beach, concealing the dunes which the rising tide would soon be covering.

Michèle de Burne, her hands clasped in her lap and a faraway look in her eyes, tried to examine her heart through a mist as pale and impenetrable as the one that hid the sands. How many times already, in her boudoir in Paris, sitting in this same posture in front of her mirror, had she wondered: Whom do I love? What do I desire? Who am I?

Aside from the pleasure of being the woman she was and from the intense need to please—which she truly enjoyed satisfying—her heart had never known more than certain fleeting interrogations. Of this she was well aware, being too accustomed to studying her face and her whole person not to observe her soul as well. Up to now she had merely indulged this vague interest in what seemed to move others but was incapable of rousing her passions, at best merely diverting her.

Yet each time she was conscious of an intimate concern for another human soul, each time a rival, disputing her claim to an admirer and rousing her possessive instincts, had made her veins glow with a touch of feverish attachment, she had found in such *false leads* a much stronger emotion than the mere pleasure of success. Yet such emotion never lasted—why was that? She wore herself out, she disgusted herself—perhaps she saw things too clearly. Everything that initially pleased her in a man, everything which moved her, disturbed her, seduced her, became all too soon familiar, banal, stale. They were so much alike, these men—without ever being the same; and none of them seemed to possess the qualities needed to keep her attention wide awake, in short, to inspire love.

And why was that? Was it their fault, or hers? Were they lacking in what she required of them, or was it she who lacked what was required in order to love? Did a woman fall in love because at last she encountered someone she felt was created for her, or did she simply fall in love because she was born with a faculty for loving? At times it seemed to her that other people's hearts must have arms like their bodies, loving arms extended to clasp and hold—and her own heart? All it had was eyes, that heart of hers.

How often she saw men, superior men, fall madly in love with women quite unworthy of them—witless, trivial girls, sometimes even without any beauty at all. Why? How? What was the mystery? So it wasn't merely a providential encounter which was responsible for this crisis of the soul but a sort of germ carried around within us all, a suddenly developing virus. She had listened to confidences, she had overheard secrets, she had even seen, with her own eyes, the sudden transfiguration that resulted from this intoxication, and she had pondered it deeply.

In the world, in the daily round of visits, of gossip, of all the little stupidities that constitute our usual diversion, that fill our ordinary emptiness, she had occasionally discovered, with envious, almost incredulous surprise, certain beings, women and men both, in whom something absolutely extraordinary had occurred. Not on the surface, not to all appearances, but she discerned it with her acute sensitivity to such concealments, she divined the miracle: in their expressions, their smiles, especially in their eyes, something ineffable, something ecstatic, something deliciously happy appeared, the soul's joy spreading through the whole body, illuminating the flesh itself, shining in the gaze.

And without knowing why, she resented them for it. Lovers had always irritated her, and she attached a certain disdain to her own secret annoyance which those whose hearts pounded with passion inspired in her. She recognized them, she believed, with an exceptional promptness and sureness of penetration. Often, in fact, she had nosed out and revealed liaisons before society had even suspected they existed.

When she thought of it, of that tender madness into which intimacy—the sight, the speech, the very thought of another being—could hurl men and women alike, and of the secret of personality by which certain hearts become so deeply troubled, she decided she was incapable of any such thing, invulnerable to it. And yet how many times, weary of everything she knew and dreaming of inexpressible desires, tormented by that stabbing lust for change and the unknown which was perhaps no more than the obscure agitation of a vague thirst for affection, she had hoped, with a secret shame born of her pride, to meet the man who would cast her, if only for a time, several months, say, into that bewitching overexcitement of her mind and heart—and of her body! For life, in such periods of emotion, must assume a strange allure of ecstasy and intoxication. Not only had she hoped for such an encounter but in a certain fashion she had even sought it out, with that indolent activity which failed to linger anywhere for long. In all these nascent involvements with the evidently superior men who had dazzled her for a few weeks, it was always with irremediable disappointments that her brief effervescences of the heart had perished. She had expected too much of such men—of their nature, of their character, of their delicacy, of their qualities. With each one of them, she had always been forced to realize that the defects of eminent men are often more salient than their virtues, that talent is a special gift, like good eyesight and good digestion, a private aptitude, an isolated endowment, with no connection to the totality of personal qualities which make relationships cordial or attractive.

But since meeting Mariolle, something different had drawn her to him. Did she love him? Was she really in love with him? Without any special prestige, certainly without fame, he had won her by his affection, by his tenderness, by his intelligence, by all the simple and genuine attractions of his person. He really had conquered her, for she thought of him constantly, constantly desired his presence; no one else in the world seemed so agreeable, so sympathetic, so indispensable. Was that love?

Certainly her soul did not report that burning emotion everyone speaks of, yet for the first time in her life she felt a sincere desire to be something more for this man than a seductive friend. Did she love him? In order to love, wouldn't the object of such an emotion have to possess exceptional attractions, different from and superior to all the others within that aureole the heart sets aglow around its favorites? Or was it enough that he should please her— please her so much that she was almost unable to do without him?

If that was the case, she loved him, or at least she was very close to loving him. After pondering the question deeply, she finally arrived at an answer: "Yes, I do love him, but I lack a certain ... impulse; it's a defect of my nature."

Yet she had certainly felt something like an impulse just now, as she saw him coming toward her on that garden terrace at Avranches. For the first time, she had felt that ineffable something which lifts us, which urges us on, which impels us toward someone; she had experienced immense pleasure walking beside him, having him close to her, burning with love for her, watching the sun set behind the shadow of Mont-Saint-Michel like some vision in a legend. Wasn't love itself a kind of legend of the soul in which some people believed instinctively, and in which others, simply by dwelling on it, ultimately managed to believe as well? Would she ultimately manage to believe in it? She had felt a strange, gentle impulse to rest her head on this man's shoulder, to be closer to him, to seek that "very close" no one ever achieves, to give him what one offers in vain and what one keeps forever: the secret intimacy of oneself.

Yes, she had felt an impulse toward him, she felt it even now, deep in her heart. Perhaps she needed only to yield to it for it to become a real emotion. She resisted too much, she argued too much, she spent too much energy opposing someone else's charm. Wouldn't it be sweet, on an evening like this, to walk under the willows along the river, and in recompense for all his passion, to offer him her lips from time to time?

A window in the villa opened. She turned her head. It was her father, who was doubtless looking for her.

She called out to him, "Aren't you asleep yet?"

He answered, "If you don't come in you'll catch cold."

Then she got up and walked toward the house. Once she was in her room, she pushed aside the curtains to watch the mists from the bay whitening in the moonlight, and it seemed to her that in her heart as well the mists were clearing in the dawn of this new tenderness.

She slept soundly, however, and it was the chambermaid who wakened her, for they were to leave early in order to take luncheon at the mount.

A carriage called for them. Hearing its wheels on the gravel drive, she leaned out the window and looked right into the eyes of André Mariolle, who had come to fetch her. She felt her heart pound, and became conscious, surprised and oppressed by the strange new impression of this palpitating muscle which makes the blood throb because someone comes into view. Just as she had that night, before falling asleep, she asked herself again, "Am I going to love him?"

Then when she came outside and their faces were a few inches apart, she realized that this man was so overwhelmed by his emotion, so deeply in love, that she really felt she should open her arms and give him her lips.

They merely exchanged a stare which left André Mariolle pale with happiness.

The carriage started moving. It was a bright summer morning, full of birdsong and the sense of beginning. They followed the coast road, crossed the river, passed through villages on a tiny gravel path which shook the travelers on the seats of the carriage. After a long silence Madame de Burne began teasing her uncle the engineer on the state of this roadway; that managed to break the ice, and the gaiety floating in the air seemed to sweeten every mind.

Suddenly, as they emerged from a hamlet, the bay reappeared, no longer golden as it had been yesterday afternoon, but gleaming with bright water which covered everything, the sands, the salt meadows, and according to the coachman, the roadway itself a little farther ahead.

Then, for an hour, they advanced at a gait which would allow the inundation to flow back into the sea.

The rows of elms and oaks between which they passed concealed, for moments at a time, the rising profile of the abbey perched on its rock, now far out at sea. Then, between two curves, it suddenly rose up again, closer than before, ever more surprising. The sun brought out the reddish tones of the church in its granite lace atop its rocky perch.

Michèle de Burne and André Mariolle contemplated the

mount, then each other, each mingling with the dawning or inflamed disturbance of their hearts the poetry of that apparition on this rosy July morning.

The conversation proceeded with friendly ease. Madame Valsaci told some tragic tales of quicksands, nocturnal dramas of the soft sand which swallows up men and cattle. Monsieur Valsaci defended the dike, attacked by the artists, or proclaimed its advantages from the point of view of uninterrupted communications with the mount, and of dune areas gained for pasture now, later for crops.

Suddenly the carriage stopped. The sea had overflowed the road. It was nothing at all, a liquid skin over the gravel surface, but it was feared that in certain places there would be quagmires, holes from which they could not emerge. They would have to wait.

"Oh, it goes down fast!" declared Monsieur Valsaci, and he pointed at the road where the thin surface of water fled away, seeming to be swallowed up by the ground, or drawn into the distance by a powerful and mysterious force.

They got out for a closer look at this strange rapid and silent retreat of the sea, and followed it step by step. Already they could see green patches of submerged herbage, faintly raised in places, and these grew larger, rounder, becoming islands. Soon these islands took on the aspect of continents separated by tiny oceans; and then at last the whole gulf became a racetrack of the returning tide as far as they could see, as if someone was drawing a long, silvery veil over the earth, an enormous ragged veil full of rips and slashes, which vanished to reveal wide meadows of low grass, without yet uncovering the blond sands which would follow them.

Everyone climbed back into the carriage, standing now for a better view. The roadway was drying as the horses walked ahead at a slow pace; sometimes the jolts made them lose their balance, and Mariolle suddenly felt Madame de Burne's shoulder against his own. At first he thought that the contact was an accidental shock, but her shoulder remained pressed against him, each jostle of the wheels hammering against the place where their bodies pressed together. Paralyzed with happiness by this unhoped-for familiarity, he dared not look at the young woman. His thoughts were in chaos—a kind of drunkenness: "Is it possible? Can it be? Are both of us losing our minds?"

Once again the horses began to trot. They had to sit down. Suddenly Mariolle felt the imperious, mysterious need to be friendly to Monsieur de Pradon, and he busied himself with flattering attentions. Almost as sensitive to compliments as his daughter, the father let himself be seduced and soon regained his smiling countenance.

At last they reached the dike: the horses were trotting toward the mount that rose at the end of the straight roadway erected on top of the sands. The Pontorson river bathed the left slope; to the right, the grassy pastures which the coachman called by some unfamiliar name had given way to still-dripping dunes. Mont-Saint-Michel loomed ever higher into the blue sky, every detail profiled very clearly now, the whole abbey bristling with grimacing gargoyles like a monstrous coiffure with which the terrified faith of our fathers had embellished their Gothic sanctuaries.

It was nearly one o'clock when they reached the inn where the luncheon had been ordered. The innkeeper, to be on the safe side, had not yet made preparations for them, and it was late before the travelers sat down to their meal, famished but immediately cheered by champagne. Everyone was soon satisfied, and two hearts were quite convinced of their happiness. Toward dessert, when the wine and the pleasure of conversation had created that contentment which sometimes envelops us at the end of a good meal, making us approve of everything, accept everything, Mariolle asked, "What do you say we stay here until tomorrow? How lovely it would be to see the mount by moonlight, and so pleasant to dine together again tonight!"

Madame de Burne accepted instantly; the other gentlemen agreed, and only Madame Valsaci hesitated, since their little boy had been left at home; but her husband reassured her, reminding her how often she had spent the night away from home. He immediately composed a telegram to the housekeeper. He had been charmed by Mariolle, who had flattered him with his approval of the dike, which he declared to be much less damaging to the general effect of the mount than people had claimed.

They got up from the dinner table to visit the abbey, taking the path through the ramparts. The town, a heap of medieval houses terraced one above the other all over an enormous block of granite bearing the abbey at its summit, was separated from the sands by a high wall. This crenellated structure rose around the old town with many turns and angles, platforms and watchtowers, creating endless surprises for the eye which discovered, at each circuit, a new stretch of the vast horizon. Everyone had stopped talking, breathing a little heavily after that long luncheon, and still astonished to see, or see again and again, this remarkable structure. In the sky above them there was a prodigious tangle of steeples, granite blossoms, arches flung from tower to tower, an incredible, enormous, yet delicate lace of architecture silhouetted on the blue sky, out of which sprang, or appeared to leap as though to take wing, a threatening and fantastic army of gargoyles with bestial faces. Between the abbey and the sea, on the mount's northern side, a wild and nearly vertical slope covered with ancient trees began where the houses ended, spreading a dark patch of green on the limitless yellow of the sands. Madame de Burne and Mariolle, who were walking ahead, stopped for the view. She was leaning on his arm, overwhelmed by a delight she had never experienced. She was climbing, weightlessly somehow, ready to climb forever with him toward that dreamlike monument and toward something else too; she would have liked this steep ascent never to end, for she felt herself to be, for the first time in her life, completely satisfied. She murmured, "My God, how beautiful this is!"

He answered, "I see nothing—except you."

And with a smile she replied, "I'm not a very poetic person, but it all seems so beautiful—I'm really very moved."

He stammered, "I'm ... I'm out of my mind with love." He felt a gentle pressure on his arm, and they walked on.

An attendant was waiting for them at the abbey door, and they entered by that splendid staircase, between two huge towers, which led them to the guardroom. And then they went from hall to hall, from courtyard to courtyard, from dungeon to dungeon, listening, astonished, delighted by everything they heard, admiring everything they saw, the crypt with its enormous pillars of such powerful beauty, supporting not only the entire choir of the upper church but also the Merveille, that wondrous three-story edifice of Gothic monuments raised one above the other, an astonishing masterpiece of medieval monastic and military architecture.

Then they came to the cloister. Their astonishment was so great that they came to a halt before this huge square meadow enclosed by the lightest, the most graceful, the most charming of colonnades of all the cloisters in the world. In double rows, the slender shafts were coiffed with delicious capitals bearing, the entire length of four galleries, an uninterrupted garland of Gothic ornaments and flowers of an infinite variety, an ever-renewed invention, the elegant yet simple fantasy of the ancient naïve artisans, who wrought their dreams and conceptions in the stone with hammer and chisel.

Michèle de Burne and André Mariolle slowly circled the entire structure, step by tiny step, arm in arm, while the others, a little weary, admired the cloister at a distance, standing near the doorway. "My God, how lovely it is!" she said, suddenly stopping.

"I don't know where I am," he answered, "nor what I'm seeing. All I know is that you're beside me."

It was then that she looked into his eyes, smiling, and murmured, "André." And he understood that she was his. They spoke no other words and walked on. The guided tour of the monument continued, but they saw no more. Yet the carved lace staircase distracted them for a moment, caught as it was in an arch flung into space between two turrets, apparently to scale the clouds; and they were again astounded upon arriving at the Madman's

Walk, a dizzying granite path winding with no parapet around the top of the last tower. "Can we walk up there?" she asked the guide.

"It's closed to the public."

She held out twenty francs. The man hesitated. The entire group, already giddy above the abyss and the immensity of space below, opposed this foolhardiness. She turned to Mariolle. "Would you like to go?"

He laughed. "I've been to scarier places." And not even looking back at the others, they set out, he climbing ahead along the narrow ledge at the edge of the abyss and she following, keeping close to the wall, eyes lowered in order not to see the yawning gulf beneath them, moved now, almost cringing with fear, clinging to the hand he held out to her; but she realized how strong he was, how unafraid, sure of his footing and his balance, and she thought, even in her terror, "Truly, this is a man." They were alone in space, as high as gulls above the sea, commanding the same horizon as those white winged creatures ceaselessly exploring the void with their tiny yellow eyes.

Feeling her tremble, Mariolle asked, "Are you feeling dizzy?"

"A little," she whispered, "but as long as I'm with you I'm not afraid." Then, turning back to her, he put his arm around her and she felt so reassured by this support that she raised her head to look into the abyss.

He was almost carrying her, and she relaxed against him, delighting in this powerful protection that took her across the heavens, and felt grateful to him—a romantic impulse—for not spoiling this aerial prowess by trying to kiss her.

But once they had rejoined their party anxiously awaiting them, Monsieur de Pradon said harshly to his daughter, "Good God, what a stupid thing to do!"

"No, Papa," she answered with conviction, "it ended well. Nothing's stupid if it ends well."

He shrugged his shoulders, and they began to walk down the mount, stopping at the porter's lodge for postcards; when they reached the inn, it was almost time for dinner. The innkeeper's wife suggested a short excursion toward the open sea. From that side, she said, the mount offered its most magnificent view.

Tired as they were, the whole party set out again, rounding the ramparts and venturing some ways into the treacherous dunes where the hard-looking surface was soft enough in places to swallow an unwary pedestrian up to the knees in golden mud.

Out here, the abbey suddenly changed its appearance. It was no longer a marine cathedral amazing distant viewers on terra firma but the warlike semblance of a feudal castle. From behind its high crenellated walls pierced with picturesque loopholes and supported by gigantic buttresses anchoring cyclopean masonry at the foot of the strange mountain, it defied the invading ocean. But Madame de Burne and André Mariolle paid little attention to all this. They thought only of themselves, caught in the trap they had set for each other, shut in that prison where they knew nothing else in the world, saw nothing more than each other.

And when they found themselves sitting in front of their full plates under the cheerful light of the lamps, they felt as though they had just awakened and realized all of a sudden that they were hungry.

They lingered over dinner, and when they left the table the moonlight was forgotten in the pleasure of conversation. Moreover no one felt like going back outside, and the subject was not mentioned. The full moon could dapple the rising tide already sliding over the sands with an almost imperceptible alarming gurgle; it could illumine the ramparts that snaked around the mount, and in the matchless setting of the infinite bay, glistening with sudden lights creeping over the dunes, it could cast romantic shadows over every turret of the abbey—they no longer cared about seeing anything at all.

It was not yet even ten when Madame Valsaci, yawning deeply, spoke of going up to bed—a proposition accepted without the slightest resistance. After a series of cheerful good-nights, each of them went to their bedroom.

Mariolle knew perfectly well that sleep was out of the question; he lit the two candles on his mantelpiece, opened his window, and surveyed the night. His whole body cringed under the torments of a futile hope. He knew she was there, close by, separated from him by two doors, and it was almost as impossible to join her as to halt that tide now inundating the whole coast. He felt the cry in his throat and in every nerve such an agony of unappeasable and futile longing that he wondered what he would do now, no longer able to endure the solitude of this evening's sterile happiness.

Gradually all the little noises fell silent in the inn and on the town's single winding road. Mariolle stayed at his window, aware only that time was passing, watching the silver layer of high tide, and still postponing the moment of going to bed, as if he had had the presentiment of some providential stroke of fortune.

Suddenly he realized that a hand was touching his lock. He turned around with a start. His door was slowly opening. A woman came in, her head veiled in white lace and her whole body swathed in one of those full dressing gowns that seem made of silk, down, and snow. She carefully closed the door behind her; then, as if she had not seen him, standing stiff and overwhelmed with joy in the bright frame of his window, she walked straight to the mantel and blew out the two candles.

2

THE PLAN was for them to meet, to say goodbye, the following morning in front of the inn. Mariolle, first to come down, was waiting for her to appear, struggling with a poignant sentiment of anxiety and happiness. What would she do? How would she act? What would become of her, and of him for that matter? What kind of affair—disastrous or wonderful—had he embarked on? She could make him into whatever she chose: an idiotic dreamer, like some opium fiend, or a martyr to infatuation. He walked beside the two carriages, for they were separating—he would finish his little trip by way of Saint-Malo, justifying his prevarication; the others would return to Avranches.

When would he see her next? Would she cut short her visit to her family or delay her return? He had an awful fear of her first glance and her first words, for he had not seen her and they had spoken almost no words during their brief embrace of the night before. She had given herself to him resolutely, but with a certain modest reserve, without manifesting much response to his caresses; then she had left, with that rapid, noiseless gait of hers, murmuring, "Till tomorrow, my friend!"

André Mariolle retained from that swift, strange occasion the imperceptible disappointment of a man who has been unable to reap the full harvest of a love he had judged ripe for the taking, and at the same time the intoxication of victory. He felt virtually assured in the hope of overcoming her last qualms.

He heard her voice and trembled. She was speaking loudly, apparently irritated by some suggestion of her father's, and when

Mariolle caught sight of her on the last step of the staircase, the tiny pout of impatience still showed on her lips. He stepped forward and when she saw him she smiled; in her suddenly calmed eyes, an affectionate light appeared which suffused her entire countenance. In the hand she suddenly and tenderly gave him, there was the unconstrained, unrepentant confirmation of the gift of herself she had given.

"Then we must part?" she asked rather than announced.

"Alas, madame, I'm afraid we must, and I regret it more than I can say."

"Well," she murmured, "it won't be for long." And then, as Monsieur de Pradon approached them, she added in a whisper, "Say that you're making a ten-day tour of Brittany, but don't go."

Just then Madame Valsaci appeared, apparently distressed. "What's this your father tells me—you're leaving the day after tomorrow? I thought you were staying at least till next Monday!"

Madame de Burne, apparently downcast, answered, "Papa always says more than he should. Every time I'm at the seaside, I get these terrible attacks of neuralgia, and I told him I should leave now in order to avoid a month in bed. But this is hardly the time to discuss the matter."

Mariolle's coachman urged him to get in his carriage in order not to miss the train for Pontorson.

"And when will you be back in Paris?" Madame de Burne asked him.

He appeared to hesitate. "I'm not really sure. I want to see something of Saint-Malo and Brest, the Pointe du Raz, Audierne, Penmarch, the Morbihan—all these famous parts of Brittany. It'll probably take me"—after a silence filled with imaginary calculations, he continued, with some exaggeration—"at least two or three weeks."

"That's quite a long trip," she answered, with a laugh. "If I have another attack like last night's, I'll be back in Paris in less than a couple of days."

Speechless with emotion, he had the impulse to shout "Thank

you!" but contented himself with a kiss—a lover's kiss on the hand she held out to him for a farewell salutation.

And after a thousand compliments, thanks, and declarations of sympathy for the Valsacis, and with Monsieur de Pradon somewhat reassured by Mariolle's announcement of his Brittany excursion, he climbed into his carriage and drove off, looking back as long as she was in sight.

He returned to Paris without delay, seeing nothing on the way, buried in a corner of his compartment on the train that night, eyes half closed, arms folded, soul dissolved in recollection, living over and over the realization of his dream. As soon as he reached home, from his first moment of solitude in the silence of the library where he worked, where he wrote, where he usually felt at peace among his books, his piano, his violin, there began within him that continuous torment of impatience which harasses insatiable hearts like a fever. Amazed that he could think of nothing, do nothing, and that he found inadequate—not only for absorbing his mind but even for immobilizing his body—the usual pastimes by which he diverted his intimate moments, reading and music, he wondered what he could do to overcome this new disturbance. A craving to go out, to walk, to bestir himself, seemed to obsess him now, physical and inexplicable, a fit of bodily agitation wrought by his state of mind—simply an instinctive and unappeasable longing to look for someone, to find someone.

He put on his overcoat, picked up his hat, opened his door, and as he ran down the stairs asked himself, "Where am I going?" And then an idea which had not yet occurred to him began to form in his mind: he had to have a place for their future encounters, somewhere secret, somewhere secluded and appealing. He began to search, walking up and down streets, avenues and boulevards, anxiously questioning concierges with their sympathetic smiles, landladies with their suggestive expressions, inspecting apartments with doubtful furnishings, and by evening returned home discouraged. At nine the next morning he resumed his quest, and by nightfall in a back street of Auteuil, at the end of a garden with three gates, he finally discovered an isolated pavilion which an upholsterer in the neighborhood agreed to furnish in two days. Mariolle chose the fabrics for the simplest varnished-pine furniture, as well as several thick carpets. The garden was looked after by a baker who lived just outside one of the gates, and an arrangement was made with the baker's wife to clean the rooms; a florist in the neighborhood would supply flowers and plants for the garden. All these preparations took him till eight that evening, and when he returned home, exhausted and satisfied, he found, with a pounding heart, a *petit bleu* on his desk:

HOME TOMORROW EVENING. INSTRUCTIONS FOLLOW. MICHE.

He had not yet written her, not knowing when she would be back in Paris and fearing a letter to Avranches might miscarry. After dinner he sat down at his desk to pour out his soul. This was a long and difficult effort, for every expression, every notion that occurred to him seemed feeble, commonplace, inadequate to transmit the delicate and passionate gratitude he wanted to convey.

The letter which arrived the next morning confirmed her return that same evening, and urged him to keep to himself for a few days, so that his Brittany excursion would seem plausible to their friends. She also suggested that he take a walk the next day, at around ten in the morning, on the terrace of the Tuileries bordering the Seine. He arrived an hour early, and wandered through the enormous park, traversed at that hour by early risers, office workers hurrying to the ministries on the Left Bank, clerks and shopgirls of all descriptions. He took a sort of philosophical pleasure in contemplating this population in thrall to the necessity of earning their daily bread, comparing himself to them at this time of day, waiting at leisure for his mistress, one of society's queens, and realizing how fortunate, how privileged a being he was, he entertained a fleeting impulse to thank the blue sky above him, for to Mariolle providence was no more than the alternation of sun and rain due to chance, artful master of days and men.

A few moments before ten o'clock, he climbed the steps to the terrace and waited for her to appear. She's sure to be late, he told himself as the clock in a nearby steeple chimed ten, and just then thought he saw her in the distance, hurrying across the gardens like a shopgirl late for work. He hesitated—could that really be she? He recognized her walk, but was surprised by her changed appearance, so modest in a dark little suit. Yet she was heading straight for the terrace stairs, as if quite familiar with these surroundings. She must like this place, he thought, maybe she comes here for walks. He watched her raise her skirt at the first stone step and almost run up the rest, and then, as he went forward to meet her, heard her murmur as they drew together, "How reckless you are! Why be so obvious? I could see you from the rue de Rivoli! Let's sit on that bench over there, behind the orangerie. That's where we'll meet next time."

There was a touch of anxiety in her warm smile, and he couldn't help asking, "Do you come here often?"

"Oh yes, I like this place a lot, and I take my morning walks here to enjoy the scenery, which as you see is well worth looking at. Besides, one never meets anybody here, while the Bois is impossible. But keep my secret."

He laughed. "You can trust me." He managed to take her hand discreetly—a little hand half hidden in the folds of her skirt—as he sighed, "I love you so much. I was going out of my mind waiting for you. Did you get my letter?"

"Yes, I did. Thank you for that. I was very moved to get it."

"Then you're not still annoyed with me?"

"No, why should I be? You're the nicest man I know."

He racked his brain for ardent expressions, phrases vibrant with gratitude and feeling. Finding none, and too moved to choose his words with any freedom, he repeated, "I love you so!"

"I asked you to meet me here," she said, "for the sake of the water and the boats. It's nothing like Avranches, but still, it's not bad."

The bench they were sitting on was near the stone balustrade along the river, and they had the place almost to themselves. Two gardeners and three nursemaids, at this time of day, were their only companions on the long terrace. Carriages rolled down the quay at their feet without their noticing, footsteps on the nearby sidewalk echoed against the wall supporting the promenade, and not yet finding what they wanted to say, they watched together the splendid Parisian landscape extending from the Île Saint-Louis and the towers of Notre Dame to the slopes of Meudon. She repeated, "How pretty it is!"

But suddenly overcome by the exalting image of their aerial exploit in the abbey tower, he exclaimed with bitter regret for that vanished emotion, "Oh dear lady, do you remember our journey on the Madman's Walk?"

"Of course I do, but now that I think of it I'm rather appalled. How dizzy I'd be if I had to do it again! I must have been drunk on the air up there, and the sun, and the sea. But look around you, isn't this splendid too, what we have in front of our eyes? I do love Paris!"

He was surprised, and had a confused presentiment that something in her that had been revealed at Mont-Saint-Michel was no longer there. "What does longitude or latitude matter, as long as I'm beside you!"

Without answering, she pressed his hand. Then, more overjoyed by this slight pressure than he might have been by the tenderest words, his heart relieved of the embarrassment that had oppressed him till now, he could finally speak. Slowly, with solemn words, he told her that he had dedicated his life to her for as long as he had a life to live, it was hers to do with as she liked.

Grateful, yet inescapably the daughter of modern doubts, captive of gnawing ironies, she smiled as she replied, "Oh don't commit yourself that far!"

He turned to look into her eyes, with a penetrating glance that was like a touch, and repeated what he had just said, only at greater length, more ardently, more poetically. Everything he had written in so many exalted letters he expressed with such a fervor of conviction that she listened to him as if in a cloud of incense, feeling herself caressed by this adoring mouth in every fiber of her being more deeply and more completely than she had ever been.

When he fell silent, she answered simply, "And I—I love you too."

They held hands like adolescents walking side by side through country lanes, dreamily watching the excursion steamers gliding past them up the river. They were alone in Paris, in the vague, immense, remote, and intimate murmur that drifted around them in this city full of the world's life, more alone than they had been at the top of the abbey tower, and for several seconds they utterly forgot that anything existed on earth except themselves. It was she who first regained the sense of reality, and of the passing time. "Shall we meet again here tomorrow?"

He reflected for a few seconds, troubled by what he was about to ask. "Yes...yes, of course...But...can't we see each other somewhere else? This *is* a secluded place...Still...anyone can come here."

She hesitated. "I know you're right...But as far as our friends are concerned, you're out of town for at least two weeks. How mysterious and appropriate for us to meet without anyone knowing you're in Paris. But I can't see you at home...it's impossible for you to come to my house. So...I don't see—"

He realized he was blushing as he interrupted. "I can't ask you to come to my place either. Couldn't there be somewhere else... Some other place...?"

She was neither surprised nor shocked, being a woman of practical reason, of enlightened logic, with no sort of false modesty. "Of course there could be—can be. It just takes a little time to plan such things."

"I have planned."

"You have? Already?"

"Yes, madame."

"And what have you planned?"

"Do you know the rue des Vieux-Champs, in Auteuil?"

"No."

"It runs from the rue Tournemine to the rue Jean-de-Saulge."

"And then..."

"And in that street, which is really just a lane, there happens to be a garden, and in that garden there is a pavilion, with gates opening onto the two streets I've just mentioned."

"And then..."

"It is that pavilion which awaits you."

She pondered this a moment and then, still without a touch of embarrassment, asked two or three questions of feminine prudence. He gave her explanations which were apparently satisfactory, for she murmured, as she stood up, "Fine. I'll come tomorrow."

"What time?"

"Three o'clock"

"I'll be waiting for you behind the door of number 7. Don't forget. Just knock as you pass by."

"Yes, I will. Goodbye, my friend. Until tomorrow."

"Tomorrow. Goodbye. Thank you. I adore you!"

They were both standing now. "Don't come with me," she said. "Stay here ten minutes, then leave along the quay."

"Goodbye."

"Goodbye."

She walked away quickly, her demeanor so discreet, so modest, so hurried, that she truly resembled one of those industrious Parisian shopgirls making her way through the streets from one honest task to the next.

He took a fiacre to Auteuil, tormented by fears the pavilion would not be ready by the next afternoon.

But he found it full of workmen. The walls were already covered with fabric, the rugs laid on the floors. In the garden, all that was left of an old park, were several fine old trees, a maze of tall bushes, two green lawns, and paths winding around the flower beds where the neighborhood florist had already planted rose-bushes, pinks, geraniums, mignonette, and a host of other plants whose growth can be hastened or delayed by careful tending, turning an uncultivated patch of ground into a blossoming bower within a day.

Mariolle was as pleased as if he had just scored another triumph in his beloved's eyes, and having obtained the upholsterer's promise that all the furniture would be in place before tomorrow noon, he rushed off to buy some knickknacks to make the interior as appealing as the garden: for the walls, photographic reproductions of famous paintings; for the mantels and tables, several Deck porcelains and other objects likely to appeal to a fastidious woman's taste. By the end of the afternoon he had squandered two months' income and took great pleasure in having done so, reminding himself that he had scrimped for a decade, not out of miserliness but because he lacked the motive for spending, which now permitted him such lordly excess.

The next morning he returned to the pavilion, supervised the delivery and placement of the furniture, hung the pictures himself, climbed stepladders to spray the hangings with perfume which he even spread on the rugs. In his feverish delight he had the impression of doing the most diverting, most delicious things he had ever done. Not a moment passed without his glancing at the clock, calculating how much time still separated him from the moment of her arrival, and he kept interrupting the workmen, convinced everything could be improved, arranging and shifting objects to appear at their best advantage.

To be on the safe side, he let all the workmen go by two o'clock and then, during the slow circuit of the minute hand on its final rounds, in the silence of that little pavilion where he awaited the greatest happiness he had ever hoped for, he savored, alone with his dream, walking back and forth from salon to bedroom, talking to himself, the truest pleasure in love he was ever to know.

Then he walked out into the garden where sunbeams fell on the grass through the foliage of the trees, suddenly illuminating a basket of roses in the most delightful way. The heavens themselves were smiling on this rendezvous. Then he stood behind the front gate, opening it every now and then for fear she might mistake the address.

Three o'clock chimed, immediately echoed by the convent steeples and factory whistles in the neighborhood. He was waiting, watch in hand now, startled when two light taps sounded against the wood to which his ear was pressed, for he had heard no footsteps in the lane.

He opened the door: it was she. She looked surprised to see him so close to her, and anxiously glanced at the houses nearby, reassured—for she certainly knew no one among the modest bourgeois living in this neighborhood. Then she inspected the garden with a satisfied curiosity, and finally she pressed the backs of both hands, from which she had just stripped her gloves, against her lover's lips and took his arm, repeating at each step: "How lovely! Imagine finding this all here! How adorable!" Noticing the bed of roses which the sun was then caressing through the branches, she exclaimed, "But it's a fairyland, my dear!" She picked a rose, kissed it, and put it in her bosom. They entered the pavilion, and she seemed so pleased he could have knelt at her feet, though in his heart of hearts he felt she might have been a little less concerned with the place and a little more with him. She explored each room, excited as a child with a new toy and evidently untroubled to find herself in this attractive tomb of womanly virtue. She marveled at the elegance of the furniture with all the satisfaction of a connoisseur whose tastes have been consulted. On her way here she had feared to find a banal love nest with stained upholstery, perhaps the worse for wear from other rendezvous. Quite the contrary, everything here was so new, so charming, quite made for her, it must all have cost Mariolle a pretty penny. He was really perfect, this man.

Turning toward him, she raised both arms in a ravishing gesture of appeal, and they embraced—one of those long kisses with closed eyes which create the strange double sensation of bliss and nothingness.

And in the undisturbed silence of this haven, they had three hours face-to-face, body to body, mouth to mouth. At last, Mariolle united the intoxication of his senses with the intoxication of his soul.

Before parting, they made another tour of the garden, then sat in lawn chairs in a secluded corner. Exuberantly André addressed her as if she were an idol who for his sake had abandoned her sacred pedestal, and she listened to him with a certain languor he had often seen in her eyes after visits from people who bored her. Yet how affectionate she remained, her face illuminated with a tender, slightly constrained smile, and holding his hand with a continuous pressure, perhaps more unconscious than deliberate.

She may not have been listening to what he was saying, for she interrupted him in mid-sentence. "I must leave this minute! I was due at the Marquise de Bratiane's at six, and I'm going to be terribly late."

He saw her tenderly to the gate he had opened for her when she came in. They embraced, and after a furtive glance down the lane she hastened away, keeping close to the garden wall. No sooner was he alone—feeling that sudden void left in us, after such embraces, by the woman who has just departed and the strange little wound inflicted on our heart by the sound of her receding footsteps—than it seemed to him he had been abandoned, solitary now as if he had received nothing from her; and he began walking along the sandy garden paths, musing on that eternal contradiction of hope and reality.

He stayed at the pavilion till nightfall, gradually becoming calmer and giving himself to her, at a distance, more absolutely than she had yielded her body in his arms; then he returned to his own apartment, dined without noticing what he was eating, and began to write her a letter.

The next day seemed long, the evening which followed interminable. He wrote to her again. How could it be that she had not answered, not communicated? A brief telegram arrived the morning of the second day, stipulating a new rendezvous tomorrow at the same time. The tiny blue page immediately cured him of this waiting sickness from which he was beginning to suffer. She came, just as she had the first time, punctual, affectionate, smiling; and their encounter in the little pavilion in Auteuil was just like the first. Mariolle, initially surprised and vaguely disappointed at not feeling between them the surge of ecstatic passion he had expected, yet even more sensually overwhelmed, gently dismissed the dream of anticipated possession in the felicity of possession obtained. He attached himself to her by caresses, a formidable link, the only one that can never be dissolved once it has taken hold deep within a man's flesh and blood. Twenty days passed, so sweet, so weightless! It seemed to him that this could never end, that he would be forever lost to the world and living for her alone, and in his sterile artist's easily influenced dreams, continually corroded by expectations, was born an impossible hope of a life forever discreet, happy, and clandestine. She came, every three days, quite readily, lured, it would seem, as much by the entertainment of their rendezvous, by the charm of the little house transformed into a paradise of blossoms, and by the novelty of a love life singularly without risk—since no one was entitled to observe it, yet so full of mystery—as she was seduced by her lover's prostrate and ever-increasing tenderness.

Then one day, she said to him, "Now, my dear friend, you must reappear. You'll come tomorrow and spend the afternoon at my house. I've announced your return."

He was horrified. "Oh, why so soon?"

"Because if people were to learn, accidentally, that you were in Paris, your presence here would be inexplicable without giving rise to...suppositions."

He acknowledged she was right and promised to come to her house the next day. A few moments later he asked her, "You're receiving company tomorrow?"

"Yes, I am. There's even going to be a little ceremony."

The news was unwelcome to Mariolle. "What kind of ceremony?"

She laughed, delighted with her triumph. "I've persuaded

Massival, by the means of the most outrageous flattery, to have his *Dido* performed at my house—no one's seen it yet. It's a poem of classical love. Marquise de Bratiane, who regards herself as Massival's sole proprietor, is furious. She'll be there, of course, since she's singing. Am I powerful, or what?"

"Will there be a lot of people?"

"Oh no, only the inner circle. You'll know almost everyone there."

"Can't I be excused from this...honor? I'm so happy in my solitude."

"Oh no, my friend. You know I count on you more than anyone else."

He could feel his heart beating. "Thank you," he said. "I'll be there."

3

"Good afternoon, my dear sir."

Mariolle noticed that it was no longer the "dear friend" of Auteuil, and the handshake was brief, a hasty squeeze of a busy, preoccupied woman in full worldly array. He walked into the salon while Madame de Burne moved toward the ripe beauty of Madame Le Prieur, whose bold décolletage and pretensions to sculptural form had granted her the slightly teasing nickname of "the Goddess." She was the wife of an academician, Department of Inscriptions and Belles Lettres.

"Ah, Mariolle," exclaimed Lamarthe, "where have you been hiding, dear fellow? We thought you were dead."

"I'm just back from a trip to Finisterre," he said, and he was enlarging on his impressions when the novelist interrupted him.

"Do you happen to know the Baroness de Frémines?"

"Just by sight; but I've heard a good deal about her. They say she's quite . . . singular."

"Absolutely unhinged, but with a certain flavor: modernity can go no further. Come, I'll introduce you." Taking Mariolle's arm, he drew him toward a young woman who was frequently compared to a doll, a pale and ravishing little creature created by the devil himself for the damnation of grown-up children with beards! Her long, narrow eyes slanted toward her temples, giving her a curiously Chinese look; a flash of blue enamel glinted between eyelids which rarely opened wide, constantly veiling this tiny creature's mystery. Her glistening hair revealed silvery highlights whenever she moved her head, and her shapely thin-lipped mouth seemed drawn by a miniaturist, then chiseled by a sculptor's delicate hand. The voice emerging from it produced crystalline vibrations, and the unexpected, mordant notions uttered with a rather icy charm, indeed the cool complexity of this neurotic gamine inspired violent agitations, if not passions, in her eager entourage. She was known all over Paris as the wittiest mondaine in society, but no one really knew what she was, what she thought, what she did. She dominated most of the men she encountered with an irresistible power, and even her husband remained an enigma: affable in his lordly way, he seemed to see nothing of what went on around him. Was he blind, indifferent, or merely easygoing? Perhaps there really was nothing to see but a cluster of eccentricities he himself certainly found entertaining. Yet all kinds of rumors circulated about this couple, some quite nasty; it was even insinuated that he profited by his wife's secret vices.

Between Madame de Burne and the baroness there were mutual, though hardly natural, attractions and fierce jealousies, periods of intimacy followed by crises of intense hostility. The two women delighted and daunted each other and sought each other out like professional duelists, each conscious of the other's skills and eager for a decisive encounter.

These were the days of Baroness de Frémines's triumph. She had just scored a great victory in the conquest of Lamarthe, whom she had plucked from her rival and ostensibly domesticated among the retinue of her acknowledged victims. The novelist appeared fascinated, charmed, and stupefied by all he had discovered in this unlikely creature, and could not resist mentioning his new mistress to everyone he met, apparently unaware that his conquest, or hers, was already a subject of lively gossip.

Just as Lamarthe was about to introduce Mariolle to the baroness, Madame de Burne's glance happened to fall on him from the other end of the salon, and the novelist smiled as he murmured in his friend's ear, "I don't think our Sovereign is pleased."

Mariolle looked up, but Madame de Burne had turned to greet

Massival, who was just entering the room. He was followed almost immediately by the Marquise de Bratiane, which caused Lamarthe to observe, "So we'll have only the second performance of *Dido*—the first must have occurred in the marquise's carriage."

And the baroness added: "Our friend de Burne's collection is truly losing its choicest jewels."

A fury, a sort of hatred of this woman flamed up in Mariolle's heart, and a sudden irritation against the entire company, against the life these people led, their ideas, their tastes, their futile pursuits, their childish diversions. Then, taking advantage of the fact that Lamarthe had leaned over to whisper something to the young woman, he turned his back and walked away.

The lovely Madame Le Prieur was standing alone, a few feet in front of him. He went to greet her. According to Lamarthe, this woman represented a dated style of beauty in their avant-garde circle. Young, tall, with regular features, her chestnut hair touched with fiery highlights, her calm, kindly manner concealing a great desire to please in the guise of a sincere and simple affection, she had acquired determined champions whom she was careful not to expose to dangerous rivals. She was said to receive only a circle of the closest intimates in which all the habitués sang her husband's praises. She and Mariolle began to chat. She immediately responded to the intelligence and the reserve of this man about whom so little was said and who seemed to offer so much more than the others.

Now the last guests were arriving: portly Fresnel, out of breath and wiping his perpetually shiny forehead with a last flourish of his handkerchief; the worldly philosopher Georges de Maltry; then, together, Baron de Gravil and Count de Marantin. Monsieur de Pradon joined his daughter in making the rounds among their guests. He paid special attention to Mariolle, but the latter grew tense as he watched Madame de Burne move around the room, lavishing her favors on everyone but himself. Twice, it was true, she had met his eyes with rapid glances that seemed to say "I'm thinking of you," but they were so fugitive that he may have misinterpreted their meaning. And then he could no longer fail to see that Lamarthe's aggressive assiduity for the Baroness de Frémines was annoying Madame de Burne. "It's only coquettish pique," he thought, "the jealousy of a *salonnière* who sees someone stealing a rare bibelot." Yet it made him wince, especially when he realized that she kept glancing at them in a furtive manner while his little conversation with Madame Le Prieur did not appear to trouble her at all. "It's because she's sure of me, and Lamarthe is getting away from her." What was love for her, their love, born only yesterday yet which had left no other idea standing in his mind?

Monsieur de Pradon asked for silence, and Massival opened the piano which Marquise de Bratiane approached, stripping off her gloves, prepared to launch into Dido's passion, when again the door opened and a young man appeared who attracted all eyes, a tall slender figure with short curly blond hair and a thoroughly aristocratic manner. Even Madame Le Prieur seemed impressed.

"Who's that?" Mariolle whispered.

"I thought you knew him. It's Count Rodolphe de Bernhaus."

"Ah! The one who had the duel with Sigismond Fabre."

"Yes."

The episode had caused a great stir. Count de Bernhaus, councillor to the Austrian embassy, a diplomat with a great future in store—an elegant Bismarck, people called him—having heard, at an official reception, some scurrilous reference to his sovereign, challenged the speaker, who happened to be a famous fencer, and killed him in the ensuing duel. Within twenty-four hours of this combat, Count de Bernhaus acquired a fame equal to Sarah Bernhardt's, with this difference: that his name was aureoled by a certain chivalric poetry. The young man was, moreover, charming, an agreeable conversationalist, and altogether distingué. Lamarthe once called him "the lion tamer of our fiercest big cats."

The count sat down beside Madame de Burne with a positively gallant air, and Massival took his place at the keyboard, which his fingers caressed for a moment or two. Almost all the guests changed their seats, drawing closer to get a good view of the singer. Lamarthe and Mariolle again found themselves shoulder to shoulder.

There was a long silence full of expectation, attention, and respect; then the pianist began with a slow, a very slow series of notes which seemed to be a sort of musical narrative: there were pauses, repetitions, sequences of little phrases, sometimes languorous, sometimes anxious, but all of a remarkable originality. Mariolle let himself dream. He saw a woman, the queen of Carthage in the prime of her ripe youth and beauty, walking slowly along the seashore. It was clear that she was suffering, that her soul was heavily burdened, and he examined Marquise de Bratiane closely.

Motionless, pale beneath heavy locks that seemed steeped in nocturnal darkness, the Italian singer stared straight ahead, blindly waiting. In her energetic, rather fierce countenance harshly punctuated by her black eyes and brows, in her entire dark and passionate being, there was something enthralling—the threat of a storm divined in lowering skies.

Massival, his long hair swaying as he raised and lowered his head, continued the poignant tale he was telling on the ivory keys. Suddenly the singer shuddered, opened her mouth, and released a wail of interminable, lacerating anguish. Not one of those clamors of tragic despair which singers release onstage with dramatic gestures, nor one of those glorious moans of deceived love which bring down the house, but an indescribable cry, emerging from the flesh not the soul, like the howl of some mangled beast, the cry of the female animal betrayed. Then she fell silent, and Massival began again, more animated, more tormented, the story of that wretched queen abandoned by her lover.

Then once more the woman's voice rang out. She was speaking now, expressing the intolerable torment of solitude, the unappeasable thirst for past caresses, and the agony of knowing he was gone forever. That warm and vibrant voice made every heart in Marquise de Bratiane's audience quiver, for this swarthy Italian woman with her shadowy hair seemed to be suffering all she described: to love or at least to be capable of loving with a furious ardor. When she finished her eyes were filled with tears, which she slowly, proudly dried. Lamarthe, shivering with artistic exaltation, leaned toward Mariolle and said, "God, how glorious she is at this moment, my dear fellow, there is a woman for you, the only one here!" Then, after a pause, he added, "Yet who knows? It may all be a musical mirage, for nothing exists but illusion! But what an art, to create such an illusion, and all illusions!"

Then there came an intermission between the first and second parts of the musical poem, during which the composer and his interpreter were fervently congratulated. Lamarthe was particularly ardent in his compliments, and sincerely so, as a man gifted with the understanding of emotion and touched by every form of the expression of beauty. The way in which he told Marquise de Bratiane what he felt when listening to her was flattering enough to make her blush; the other women who heard his praise felt some resentment, and Lamarthe himself may not have been unconscious of the effect his words were having. When he returned to his seat, he noticed that Count Rodolphe de Bernhaus was sitting next to Baroness de Frémines. She appeared to be confiding secrets to him, and both were smiling as if this intimate moment delighted them equally. Mariolle, feeling increasingly gloomy, leaned against a door. The novelist walked over to him. Fresnel, Georges de Maltry, Baron de Gravil, and Count de Marantin had surrounded Madame de Burne, who was serving tea, with a ring of worshippers. Lamarthe pointed this out sarcastically to his friend, adding: "A ring without a real jewel, however, and I'm sure she'd give every one of those rhinestones for the one diamond that's missing."

"Which diamond is that?" Mariolle asked.

"Bernhaus of course, the handsome, irresistible, incomparable Bernhaus, for whom this little party is being given and for whom she performed the miracle of persuading Massival to put on his Florentine *Dido* here in the first place."

André Mariolle, though incredulous, felt a pang of intense dismay. "Has she known him long?"

"Oh no, ten days at the most. But she has exerted herself during this brief campaign, and revealed herself to be a great strategist. If you'd been here, you'd have had a good laugh."

"Why is that?"

"She met him for the first time at Baroness de Frémines's. I was there for dinner that night. Bernhaus is quite at home there, as you can see—just look at him now! And the moment their introductions were made, our lovely friend Burne marshaled her forces to conquer the one and only Austrian. She succeeded then and she'll succeed now, even though the little Frémines far surpasses her in impudence, in real indifference, and probably in perversity as well. But our friend Burne is more of a woman, more of a modern woman, you know what I mean, irresistible in the artifice of seduction which has replaced the old power of natural charm. I shouldn't even call it artifice, it's really an aesthetic, the deep sense of a feminine aesthetic. All her power is there. She knows herself very well—because she pleases herself more than anyone else, and she's never wrong about the best way to conquer a man and to show herself off to the best advantage."

Mariolle protested. "I think you're exaggerating: with me she's always been quite simple!"

"Because simplicity's the trick that works for you. I'm not saying a word against her, you know. I think she's superior to all her kind. But they're not real women."

A few chords from the piano silenced them, and Marquise de Bratiane sang the second part of the poem, in which she proved to be all physical passion and sensual despair: a splendid Dido.

But Lamarthe did not take his eyes off the colloquy between Baroness de Frémines and Count de Bernhaus. The moment the piano's last vibrations were drowned in applause, Lamarthe went on impatiently, as if he were continuing an argument with some adversary. "No, they're not women at all. Even the honest ones are unconscious bitches. The more I see of them, the less I feel that gentle intoxication a real woman gives a man. Oh, they intoxicate us all right, but it's all in the nerves—they're adulterated. Tasty, but nothing like good old wine. Look here, my dear fellow, a women is created for two things in this world, the only ones that can reveal what her true virtues are, her excellent qualities: love and children. I sound like Monsieur Prudhomme. But these creatures are incapable of love, and they don't want to have children. When they do it's a misfortune, then a burden. The truth is, they're monsters."

Startled by the writer's violent tone and by the rage that glistened in his eyes, Mariolle asked him, "Then why do you spend half your life with them?"

"Why? Why? Because they interest me, that's why! Besides . . . besides, would you forbid a doctor to enter the hospital to examine the sick? These creatures are my clinic!" This notion seemed to have calmed him down. He added: "And then I adore them because they're so much of our moment. Actually, I'm no more a man than they're women. Whenever I get attached to one, I enjoy analyzing what repels me about her, with all the curiosity of a chemist who poisons himself in order to discover an antidote." After a silence he continued. "That way I'll never be really caught. I can play their game as well as they do, maybe better, and it helps me write—nothing I do helps them with whatever it is that they do. Stupid creatures! Failures, all of them, delicious failures whose only achievement, if they're sensitive at all, is to die of disappointment as they grow old."

Listening to Lamarthe, Mariolle felt himself succumbing to a depression like the kind produced by an endless succession of dark rainy days. He realized that on the whole the novelist wasn't mistaken, but couldn't bear to admit that he was entirely right. With some irritation, Mariolle took up the argument, not so much to defend women as to locate the cause of their disenchanted mobility in contemporary literature. "In the days when poets and novelists exalted women and made them dream," he said, "they sought and believed they found in their lives the same

things that their hearts responded to in books. Today you eliminate all the poetic trappings in order to reveal nothing but disil-
lusioning realities. And when there's no love left in books, my
dear fellow, there's no love in life. You writers invented the ideal,
and your readers believed in your invention. Now you're just reality merchants, and in your wake they've begun to believe in universal vulgarity."

Lamarthe, ever eager for a literary argument, was about to
launch into another dissertation when Madame de Burne came
toward them. She was really at her best, dressed to delight the eye
and with that provocative expression which gave her a certain
combative quality. She sat down. "This is what I like," she exclaimed, "catching two men talking who aren't trying to impress
me. Besides, you're the only two men here who know how to talk.
What are you arguing about?"

Lamarthe, without the slightest embarrassment and deliber-
ately adopting a tone of gallant raillery, revealed the question at
issue. Then he repeated his own arguments with a verve accentu-
ated by the desire to show himself to advantage, the desire which
rouses all men who seek success in a lovely woman's presence, as
he remarked. Madame de Burne entered into the argument
straightway, and warming to the subject, took up the defense of
women with a good deal of wit and relevance. Several observations, intentionally incomprehensible to the novelist, concerning
the faithfulness and attachment of which even the most suspect
woman might be capable, made Mariolle's heart throb, and when
she left them to join Baroness de Frémines, who had stubbornly
kept Count de Bernhaus beside her, Lamarthe and Mariolle, dazzled by her revelations of feminine grace and wisdom, declared to
each other that here incontestably was an exquisite woman.

"Just look at her!" the writer exclaimed.

It was the grand passage at arms. What were they talking
about now, the Austrian count and the two women? Madame de
Burne had arrived at precisely the moment when the overex-
tended tête-à-tête of two persons, even when they are taken with

each other, becomes monotonous; and she broke in by repeating in high dudgeon what she had just heard Lamarthe say. All of which could certainly apply to Baroness de Frémines and her most recent conquest, uttered in the presence of an exceptionally quick-witted man likely to grasp the entire situation. Once again the argument flared up concerning the eternal question of love, and Madame de Burne beckoned to Mariolle and Lamarthe to join them, and as their voices grew more insistent, she urged the others to join in. An impassioned general discussion followed, each partisan offering his or her cleverest riposte, though Madame de Burne managed to be the subtlest and most amusing of them all, allowing traces of perhaps factitious sentiment to tinge her comical reasoning, thereby appearing indisputably livelier, cleverer, and prettier than she had ever been.

4

As SOON as Mariolle had left Madame de Burne, the incisive charm of her presence vanished. He felt in and around himself, in his flesh, in his soul, in the air he breathed, in the entire world a sort of disappearance of that joy in being alive that for some time had animated and sustained him.

What had happened? Nothing, virtually nothing. She had been charming to him at the end of her party, telling him in one or two glances: "For me you're the only person here." And yet he felt she had shown him things he would have preferred not to know. That too was nothing, virtually nothing; and yet he remained stunned, like a man who learns of some shady activity on the part of his mother or father: he discovered that during those twenty days—twenty days he had believed to be completely dedicated, by her as by himself, to the emotions, so new and so intense, of their budding intimacy—that she had resumed her old ways, made visits, laid plans, recommenced those hateful flirtations, renewed those duels with her rivals, pursued men, received certain compliments with gratitude, and deployed all her charms and graces for others besides him.

Already! She had done all that already! Oh, later on he wouldn't have been at all surprised. He knew the world, he knew women's ways, especially where feelings were concerned, nor would he ever have made—being intelligent enough to understand such things —excessive demands, nor plagued her with easily hurt feelings. She was born to certain social usages, and besides she was so lovely, made to please, to receive homage and hear compliments.

Among all the men she knew, she had chosen him, had given herself to him, boldly, royally. He would have remained, he *remained* the grateful servant of her whims, the resigned spectator of her life as a beautiful woman. But he was suffering now, in that dark cave of the heart where a man's delicate sensibilities lie hidden.

No doubt he was wrong—he had always been wrong the same way as long as he could remember. He was too emotionally vulnerable for the world he lived in, too thin-skinned. Hence the sort of isolation he lived in, for fear of contacts, collisions. He was wrong, for such collisions are almost always caused by what we cannot endure or even acknowledge in others, a nature quite different from our own. He knew this was so—how often he had observed it! Yet he could not change the vibration to which his soul was tuned.

Certainly he could not blame Madame de Burne for the way he was suffering now; if she had kept him away from her salon and hidden from her circle during those days of happiness she had given him, it was to avoid prying eyes, to prevent suspicion, to belong to him all the more completely in the future. Then why this pain gnawing at his heart? Why indeed? Because he had believed she was entirely his, and just realized, just guessed that he would never embrace for his very own the ever-extending surface of this woman who belonged to everyone.

Moreover he knew perfectly well that life consists of approximations, and until now he had resigned himself to the fact, concealing his dismay at inadequate satisfactions under a mask of deliberate reserve. But this time he thought he had gained what he had always dreamed of, always sought: complete possession of a woman he loved. Such completeness is not of this world.

His evening had been a melancholy one, and he consoled himself with rationalizations for the painful impressions he had brought home with him. When he went to bed, those impressions deepened instead of diminishing, and since he never left his memories unexplored, he traced his new heartsickness back to its remotest sources. His wounded feelings faded and revived like gusts of icy wind, wakening in his new love a suffering that was still faint, still remote, but as unsettling as those twinges of neuralgia produced by a sudden draft, harbingers of spasms of horrible pain.

He realized that he was jealous, no longer merely as an idealizing lover but as a possessive male. As long as he hadn't seen her in the company of men, of *her* men, this sentiment had not occurred to him, only vaguely anticipated perhaps, but imagined as different, very different from what it would become. In discovering the mistress he had supposed to be entirely with him during those days of secret and frequent encounters, that time of first embraces altogether given up to isolation and ardor—in discovering her to be so amused, perhaps even more than before she had given herself to him, amused and indeed excited by all her old and trivial coquetries, squandering her person on anyone and everyone (which could not have left much energy to devote to her secret choice), he discovered himself jealous carnally even more than in mere concept, jealous not in some vague way, as if suffering from a low fever, but quite precisely: he did not trust her.

At first he doubted her instinctively, by an impulse flowing in his veins rather than in his mind, the almost physical discomfort of a man uncertain of his lover. And having doubted her in that fashion, he began to have suspicions.

What was he to her, after all? A first lover, or the tenth? The immediate successor of Monsieur de Burne, or the successor of Lamarthe, of Massival, of Georges de Maltry, and perhaps the predecessor of Count de Bernhaus? What did he know about her? That she was a lovely woman, more elegant than any other, intelligent, subtle, witty, but capricious, easily bored, wearied, disgusted, supremely self-absorbed, and insatiably flirtatious. Had she had a lover—or lovers—before him? If not, would she have given herself so brazenly? Where had she learned to open his bedroom door, at night, in an inn? Would she have ventured so readily to the pavilion in Auteuil? Before appearing there she had merely asked a few questions that would occur to any experienced and vigilant woman. He had answered them as a circumspect man, accustomed to such encounters; and she had immediately said "Yes," confident, reassured, most likely informed by previous adventures.

With what discreet authority she had knocked at that little door behind which he was waiting so shyly, his heart pounding! How coolly she had walked in, without showing any emotion, solely concerned whether she might be recognized by someone in the house next door! How quickly she had made herself at home in that suspect pavilion he had rented and furnished for their lovemaking! What woman, however bold, superior to conventions, disdainful of moral prejudice, would have been so calm about an encounter with a lover at her first rendezvous?

Mental scruples, physical hesitations, the instinctive trepidation experienced on venturing into new surroundings—wouldn't she have felt and shown such things, unless she were more or less practiced in these erotic adventures, or if the familiarity of such occasions had not already worn her native modesty somewhat thin?

Tormented as if by insistent, intolerable fever brought on by such hateful thoughts, Mariolle tossed and turned in his bed, struggling like a man dragged over a precipice by the chain of his suspicions. Sometimes he tried to sever the links between these accusations, seeking, finding, and relishing sensible and reassuring arguments; but a seed of fear had been planted, and he could not halt its growth.

Yet what was there to reproach her with? Nothing except not being precisely like himself, not understanding life as he did, not having a heart perfectly in tune with his own.

As soon as he woke the next morning, the craving to see her again, to fortify his confidence in her by her presence, became a sort of hunger, and he waited for the right moment to make his first official visit. When she saw him in the doorway of her little drawing room where she was writing letters, she stood up and came toward him with outstretched hands. "Oh good afternoon, dear friend!" she cried, her happiness so evident and so genuine that all the odious suspicions still darkening his mind evaporated at her welcome.

Then he sat down beside her and immediately began telling her how much he loved her now, for it was no longer the same as before. Tenderly he explained to her that in a man's world there are two kinds of lovers: those whose fierce desire fades with the first night's triumph, and those whom possession captures and enslaves, for in them sensual fulfillment, mingling with the inexpressible appeals a man's heart sometimes makes to the woman he desires, generates a complete and tormenting servitude of love. Tormenting? Yes, invariably, however happy his love may have made him, for nothing ever satisfies, even during the most intimate hours, the need for *her* such a lover carries in his heart.

Madame de Burne listened to him, charmed, grateful, and enthralled at hearing such words—enthralled as by an actor who performs powerfully in a role that wakes an echo in our own life. There was indeed an echo, the disturbing echo of a sincere passion, but not one that cried out within her. Yet she felt glad to have caused such feelings, glad to have caused them in a man capable of expressing them so well, a man who certainly pleased her greatly, whom she was genuinely fond of and whom she needed more and more, not for her body, not for her flesh, but for that mysterious feminine self so greedy for tenderness, for homage, for conquest—so glad that she wanted to embrace him, to give him her lips, to give him everything if only he might go on worshipping her like that.

She answered him without pretense and without prudery, with the profound tact certain women possess, assuring him that he too had made, in her own heart, great progress. And in that little drawing room where it so happened that day that no one came until it was growing dark, they remained alone together talking to each other about the same thing, caressing each other with words which failed to have the same meaning for their two souls.

The lamps were just being brought in when Marquise de Bratiane appeared. Mariolle stood up to leave, and as Madame de

Burne was accompanying him to the outer salon, he asked her, "When shall I see you *there*?"

"Will Friday do?"

"Of course. What time?"

"The same time. Three o'clock."

"Till Friday then. Goodbye. I adore you!"

During the two days of waiting which separated him from this meeting, he discovered, he experienced the sensation of emptiness he had never known before. A woman was missing from his life, and except for her what else existed? And since that woman was not far away, was altogether accessible, and nothing but the merest social convention kept him from being with her at any moment, even from living quite close to her, he fretted in his solitude, in the interminable flow of moments that pass so slowly, against the absolute impossibility of doing such a very simple thing.

On Friday he arrived at the pavilion three hours ahead of time; but it gratified him to wait where she would come, relieved his exasperation after having already suffered so terribly from mentally awaiting her in places where she would not appear. He installed himself near the garden door well ahead of the longed-for three chimes from the nearby steeple, and as soon as he heard them he shivered with impatience. Quarter past three struck. Sliding his head around the doorframe, he glanced cautiously up and down the lane, which was completely deserted. The minutes became a slow torment. Over and over he looked at his pocket watch, and when the minute hand marked the half hour, he had the distinct impression of having stood in that one place an incalculable interval. Suddenly he heard a light sound on the cobblestones, and the little taps of a gloved finger made him forget his anguish: she was here, and he was overwhelmed with gratitude.

"Am I very late?" she asked, a little out of breath.

"No, not very."

"You can't imagine what it was like. I almost couldn't come. My house was full, and I had no idea how to get rid of all those people. Tell me, are you here under your own name?"

"No, why do you ask?"

"So I can send you a message if I'm unable to come."

"My name is Monsieur Nicolle."

"Fine. I won't forget. Lord how lovely it is here in this garden!" The flowers, coddled, replaced, and multiplied by the gardener who discovered that his client paid liberally without haggling, embellished the lawn in five brilliant fragrant beds.

She stopped near a bench in front of a huge basket of heliotrope. "Let's sit here for a while. I have a very funny story for you." And she launched into a piece of gossip so fresh that she was still excited by it herself. Apparently in a fit of jealousy Madame Massival, the artist's former mistress whom he had married some time ago, had burst into Marquise de Bratiane's house during a party while the marquise was singing, accompanied by the composer. There had been a terrible scene, to the Florentine's exasperation and the guests' surprise and delight. Massival struggled to eject his wife, who was slapping his face, pulling his beard, biting him, and tearing his clothes. He was quite paralyzed by all this aggression, until Lamarthe and two servants, summoned by the racket, gradually managed to free him from this Fury's claws and fangs, but calm was restored only after the couple's departure. And following this incident the musician was nowhere to be seen, while the novelist, who had witnessed and to some degree participated in the scene, described it all over town in the most amusing terms imaginable.

Madame de Burne was quite agitated by the affair, so much so that she could talk of nothing else. Soon the constantly recurring names of Massival and Lamarthe began to irritate Mariolle. "You heard this just now?"

"Yes, about an hour ago, not even an hour..."

Somewhat bitterly he mused, "And that's why she's late." Then he asked, "Shall we go in?"

Docile and somewhat distractedly she murmured, "Oh, of course..."

When, an hour later, she had left him, for she claimed to be in a great hurry, he returned alone to the little pavilion and sat in a low chair in their bedroom. The impression that he had no more possessed this woman than if she had not come at all left a sort of black void in the center of his being into which he stared as if it were bottomless. There was nothing to be seen, and nothing to be understood. If she hadn't quite escaped his kisses, she had at least managed to evade the embrace of his tenderness by a mysterious absence of any desire to belong to him. Not that she had refused him, she had not avoided him—she had come to him. But he felt that her heart had not come with her. It had remained elsewhere, at a great distance, sauntering elsewhere, diverted by trifles.

It was then he realized that he already loved her with his senses as much as with his soul, perhaps more. The disappointment of his futile caresses roused a furious desire to run after her, to bring her back, to take her once again. But why? What would be the use, since the attentions of that fickle mind were elsewhere today? So he would have to wait for the days and hours when the whim of being in love would occur to this changeable mistress.

Slowly, lethargically he returned home with heavy steps, his eyes fixed on the sidewalk; he was tired of living. And he recalled that they had made no engagement for the future, neither at her house nor elsewhere.

5

UNTIL THE beginning of winter she was more or less faithful to their trysts. Faithful, not punctual.

During the first three months she came anywhere from three-quarters of an hour to two hours late. Since the autumn showers forced Mariolle to wait shivering under an umbrella, his feet in the mud behind the garden door, he had had a sort of little wooden vestibule built there, in order to wait for her without catching cold each time they met. The trees were bare now. Instead of roses and all the other flowers, the beds were full of pink, white, lavender, yellow, and russet chrysanthemums which added to the moist air, already heavy with the melancholy smell of rain on dead leaves, their slightly acrid, balsamic odor, a little melancholy as well: the special scent of the late season's tall, noble blooms. Just inside the pavilion door, the delicate shades of several rare species, hypertrophied by the gardener's art, formed a huge Maltese cross, and Mariolle could no longer pass this bed of new and surprising varieties without a pang at the thought that this blossoming cross seemed to mark a grave.

How well he knew them now, those long waits in the kiosk behind the door. Rain soaked the thatch covering the little roof, then dripped down the plank walls, and at each station in this Chapel of Anticipation, the same reflections would occur to him and he would repeat the same arguments, regurgitating the same hopes, the same anxieties, the same discouragements. This was an unforeseen, incessant struggle, a moral combat, desperate and exhausting, with an opponent which perhaps did not exist: the tenderness of this woman's heart. How bizarre their encounters were!

Sometimes she would arrive laughing, eager to talk, and sit down without taking off her hat and gloves, without raising her veil, without even giving him a kiss. More often than not, nowadays, it did not occur to her to give him a kiss. Her head was filled with a host of captivating preoccupations, more captivating than offering her lips to a lover in the grip of a desperate passion. He would sit down beside her, his heart and his mouth full of ardent words which never emerged; he listened to her, he answered, and while appearing quite interested in what she was telling him, he sometimes tried to take her hand which she abandoned to him almost unconsciously, in a calm and friendly gesture.

At other times she would seem more tender, more attentive; but he, fixing her with intent, anxious eyes, the eyes of a lover incapable of conquering her entirely, realized at once that this comparatively affectionate mood resulted from the lack of any livelier preoccupation—on such days her mind was not engaged, not distracted by anyone or anything.

Moreover her continual lateness convinced Mariolle how little store she set by their meetings. One hurries toward what one loves, toward what pleases, toward what attracts; one can always postpone a less than appealing engagement. A singular comparison with himself constantly occurred to him: in summer the desire for a cold plunge made him hurry his morning ablutions and his daily visit to the baths, while during icy weather he found any number of little things to do at home, so that he always managed to arrive an hour later than usual. For her their Auteuil meetings were the equivalent of his winter *douches*.

For some time now she had spaced out their meetings, postponing them from one day to the next, sending messages at the last possible moment, apparently eager to find excuses for cancellations which never troubled her, though they caused him real mental and physical anguish. If she had appeared to cool off, or had shown some exasperation with his apparently ever-increasing passion, he might have been irritated, then offended, then discouraged, and finally appeased. But on the contrary she seemed more attached to him than ever, flattered by his love and more eager to sustain it, though without responding to it except by certain friendly preferences which were beginning to make her other admirers jealous.

At her own house she could never see him enough, and the same telegram that would announce a difficulty for Auteuil would always beg him to come for dinner or to spend an hour with her in the evening. At first he had interpreted such invitations as a form of making amends, but soon he was compelled to realize that she really loved seeing him—more than all the others, that she truly did need him, needed his worshipful language, his lover's glances, his enveloping affection, and his presence, like a discreet caress. She needed him the way an idol, to become a true deity, needs the prayers of the faithful. In an empty shrine, the figure is no more than a piece of carved wood; yet should even one believer enter the sanctuary, prostrate himself, and worship, groaning with fervor, intoxicated with faith, the idol becomes the equal of Brahma, of Allah, of Jesus. Every authentically loved being is a kind of god.

Madame de Burne felt herself specifically born to the role of a fetish, created for that mission assigned to women by nature—to be worshipped and pursued, to triumph over men by beauty, by grace, by coquetry and charm. She was indeed a sort of human goddess, delicate, disdainful, and demanding, worshipped by men whose love enthroned and deified her, like so much incense.

Yet she manifested her affection and her distinct preference for Mariolle almost openly, unconcerned about gossip, and perhaps with the secret desire to exasperate and inflame the others. One could virtually never visit her these days without finding him there, usually installed in a big armchair Lamarthe called "the pulpit"; and she took sincere pleasure in remaining alone with him for whole evenings, chatting and listening to him talk.

This intimate life Mariolle had revealed to her, this constant contact with an enlightened, informed mind that now was *hers*, of which she was as much the owner as of the little bibelots scattered about on her tables—all this delighted her. And gradually, too, she shared with him a good deal of her own life, of her notions, her secret self, in those affectionate confidences that were as sweet to make as to receive. With him she felt more truly free, more sincere, more candid, more intimate than with the others, and for that reason she loved him more. And she experienced that feeling, so dear to women, of truly bestowing something, confiding to someone all she could give of herself, which she had never done. For her this was a great deal, but for him little enough. He expected, he had always hoped for the great definitive abandonment of the lover who yields her soul amid caresses. Caresses she seemed to regard as futile, embarrassing, rather painful. She submitted to them, not unfeeling but soon tired, and no doubt such lassitude gently shifted to ennui. Even the most delicate, the slightest seemed to weary, to weaken her. When, as they talked, he took one of her hands to kiss her fingers, keeping them a moment, one after the next, between his lips, like bonbons, but barely breathing on them, she seemed eager to pull away, and along the whole length of her arm he felt a secret effort of withdrawal. When, at his visit's end, he pressed on her neck, between the collar of her gown and the gold hairs of her nape, a long kiss seeking the scent of her body beneath the folds of cloth, she always made a tiny movement away from him, her skin retracting almost imperceptibly beneath that alien mouth.

All this he felt as so many knife thrusts, and he went away with wounds which continued to bleed in the solitude of his desire. Why hadn't she acknowledged at least that fervent interval almost every woman experiences after the deliberate and willing submission of her body? Often it is brief, followed by fatigue and then disgust, but for it not to exist at all, not for a day, not for an hour—that had to be exceptional. Such a mistress made him not a lover but a sort of intelligent associate of her life.

Yet what did he have to complain of? Women who gave all of

themselves may not have had so much to give. He didn't complain: he was afraid. Afraid of the next man, the one who would suddenly appear, tomorrow or the next day, an artist, an officer, an actor, a duke, someone or other born to please her for no better reason than because he was *that man*, the one who would infect her for the first time in her life with the imperious desire to open her arms. Already he was jealous of the future, as he had momentarily been jealous of the unknown past, and just when all this young woman's intimates were beginning to be jealous of him. They would be talking about him to one another, and making even in her hearing quite discreet and obscure allusions. According to some, he was her lover. Others agreed with Lamarthe, claiming that she was amusing herself, in her usual way, by driving him crazy in order to annoy and exasperate *them*, nothing more than that. Her father was upset and made certain remarks to her which were coldly received; and the more she noticed the stories spreading around her, the more she persisted in showing her preference for Mariolle, bizarrely contradicting her habitually prudent existence. He, however, grew anxious hearing these suspicious murmurs and spoke to her about them.

"What does it have to do with me?" she said.

"But if you really loved me—"

"Don't I love you, my friend?"

"Yes and no. You love me well enough here at home, and not so well elsewhere. I'd prefer it the other way around for myself, and even for you."

She began to laugh, murmuring, "I'm doing the best I can."

"If you only knew," he retorted, "what I go through trying to make you love me. Sometimes it's as if I'm trying to kiss a mouthful of air—or maybe it's ice, melting away in my arms."

She made no reply, clearly finding his words distasteful and assuming that absent expression that had become so familiar to him at Auteuil. He dared not pursue the subject, gazing at her the way visitors to museums examine precious objects that cannot be taken away, however tempting they seem.

His days, his nights now seemed to him no more than so many hours of suffering, for he lived with the fixed idea and, even more than the idea, the fixed emotion that she was his and yet not his at all, vanquished and free, captive and impregnable. He lived in her vicinity, quite close to her, without reaching her, and he loved her with all the unsatisfied covetousness of his body and soul. As at the beginning of their liaison, he wrote her letters. There had been a time when he had successfully besieged her virtue with pen and ink; with the same means he might once again overcome this latest intimate and secret resistance. Visiting her less frequently, he repeated in almost daily letters the inanity of his besieging love. Now and again, when he had been really eloquent, impassioned, agonized, she would answer; her letters, outrageously dated "Midnight," "One AM," "Two AM," were bright, terse, well thought out, fond and encouraging, and utterly disheartening. She argued well, wittily, even whimsically. But however many times he read them, they were always merely good-humored, gracefully rewarding his male vanity; nothing seemed to come from the heart. They offered no more than the kisses she gave him in the pavilion at Auteuil.

He struggled to understand why. And eventually, by reading them over until he knew her letters by heart, he managed to find the reason, for it is always by their writing that one arrives at the truth of people. Language dazzles and deceives because it is masked by faces, because we see it emerging from the lips, because lips please and eyes beguile. But words on paper, black on white, reveal the naked soul.

A man, by rhetorical artifice, by professional skill, by the habit of wielding the pen for all the business of life, often succeeds in disguising his true nature in impersonal prose, whether utilitarian or literary. But a woman writes only to speak of herself and puts a little of herself in each word. Most women are strangers to the ruses of style and utterly betray themselves in the innocence of their expressions. Mariolle recalled the memoirs and correspondence of celebrated women he had read: how clearly they showed themselves to be what they were, the précieuse, the wit, the sensitive soul! What struck him most about Madame de Burne's letters was the complete absence of sensibility. This woman thought, she never felt. He called to mind other letters—how many he had received. Those from a little bourgeoise he had met on a trip and who had loved him for three months, writing him delicious, vibrant missives, filled with original and unexpected turns of phrase. He had been truly amazed by the lively elegance and the colorful variety of her sentences. Where did this talent come from? From her capacity for feeling, nothing else. A woman does not tinker with the terms she uses. Emotion casts them directly into her mind; she does not search through dictionaries. When she has strong feelings, she finds, without study or rehearsal, in the fluid sincerity of her nature, appropriate expression for them.

It was the sincerity of his mistress's nature he was trying to discover in the lines she had written him—or between the lines. Her text was all very friendly, very fine, but couldn't she have done better than *fine*? Surely he had found more to say to *her*—words like burning coals had spoken for him.

When his valet brought the mail, he would sift through the pile of envelopes for the handwriting he craved, and when he recognized it, an involuntary wave of emotion broke over him; his heart began pounding. He seized that one envelope, studied the address once again, then tore it open. What would she say this time? Would she use the verb "love" without spoiling it by adding "very much"? Could there be much or little to add to "love," if it was really love? Who can say a person loves "well" or "badly," a lot or a little—were there such proportions in love? A human being loves, nothing more, nothing less, the meaning cannot be completed beyond the word—nothing further can be imagined, nothing said beyond those letters in that order. A single syllable, but it is everything: it becomes the body, the soul, life itself. You feel it like the heat of your blood, you breathe it like the air in your lungs, you bear it in yourself like Thought, for it turns into the One Thought. Nothing else exists. It's not a word at all but an ineffable state, represented by some letters. And whatever you do, you do nothing, you feel nothing, you taste nothing, you suffer nothing as it was before. Mariolle had become the prey of that tiny verb, and his eyes ran over the lines, searching for the revelation of an affection like his own, and of course he found reason to whisper to himself "She loves me very much," but never to cry out "She loves me!" In Madame de Burne's correspondence she continued the pretty little romance begun at Mont-Saint-Michel, yes, that *roman*, that charming novel would be continued in the Paris mail, it would be a *love story*, it was not love.

When he had finished reading and rereading the letter, he would shut those beloved and heartbreaking pages in a drawer and collapse in an armchair in which he had already spent many hard hours.

After a considerable interval, Madame de Burne answered less frequently, doubtless tired of inventing new phrases and repeating the same sentiments. Moreover she was passing through a sort of social crisis whose approach Mariolle had registered by that increased suffering which even the slightest disagreeable incidents inflict upon hearts in pain.

It was a winter of mundanities. Paris was in the grip of a pandemic of parties; all night long, fiacres and coupés rolled up and down the avenues, bearing to their destinations behind rolled-up windows the pale apparitions of extravagantly gowned women. Everyone seemed to be celebrating something, and the relish for diversion had suddenly spread to all classes of society; Madame de Burne did not escape the contagion.

It all began for her with a triumph she had scored at a ballet performed at the Austrian embassy. Count de Bernhaus had managed to establish relations between Madame de Burne and the ambassador's wife, the Princess von Malten, whose seduction by Madame de Burne was as complete as it had been sudden. In no time she became the princess's intimate friend and thereby rapidly extended her connections in diplomatic circles and at the loftiest level of aristocratic society. Her grace and charm, her elegance, and the vivacity of her conversation soon established her success at every function at which she appeared; her presence at parties became an index of fashion, and in no time ladies possessing the grandest titles in France were insisting on being taken to at her at-homes. Every Monday a long row of carriages emblazoned with armorial bearings lined up along the sidewalks of the rue du Général Foy, and Madame de Burne's servants frequently confused duchesses with marquises, countesses with baronesses, in announcing these great names at the door of her salon.

She was intoxicated by her success. Compliments, invitations, extravagant flattery, the realization that she had become a chosen being, one of the elect whom Paris acclaims, adulates, worships as long as its enthusiasm lasts, the pleasure of being admired, sought after, courted on all sides, caused an acute paroxysm of snobbery in her very soul.

Her clan of artists attempted to resist, and this revolution produced an intimate alliance among her old friends. Fresnel himself was enlisted among them and became a force in the troupe, at whose head was Mariolle, for all acknowledged his influence over her and her friendship for him. But he could only watch her being whirled away in this flattering cyclone of worldly popularity, the way a child watches his red balloon disappear once he has let go of its string.

It seemed to him she was escaping into an elegant, gaudy crowd, dancing away, far from that strong secret happiness he had so hoped for, and he was jealous of it all—men, women, things even. He detested the kind of life she was leading, the people she was seeing now, the parties she was invited to, the music, the theaters, parceling out her hours, absorbing her days and her nights: only a few hours remained for the intimacy they once had. His resentment was so fierce that his health began to suffer, and the set of his ravaged features made her ask him, "What's the matter with you? You're so thin I hardly know you—"

"The matter is I love you too much."

She shot him a grateful glance. "No one can love too much, my friend."

"Are you telling that to me?"

"Of course I am. Don't you believe me?"

"Don't you understand that I'm sick? Sick to death of loving you to no purpose."

"First of all, you hardly love me to no purpose. And no one dies of such things. You must have noticed that all our friends are jealous of you, which proves I'm not treating you too badly, all things considered."

He took her hand. "You don't understand me."

"Yes I do. I understand you very well."

"You hear the desperate appeal I keep making to your heart?"

"Yes, I hear it."

"And…?"

"And…it pains me a lot, because I love you a great deal."

"So?"

"So you keep telling me: 'Be like me; think like me, feel like me, express yourself like me!' But I can't, my poor friend. I am what I am. You've got to accept me as God made me, since I've given myself to you completely, and I haven't the slightest desire to take myself back. You're dearer to me than anyone I know."

"You don't love me."

"I love you with all the strength of the love that is in me. If it isn't any stronger, is that my fault?"

"If I felt sure of that, I might be able to be satisfied."

"What does that mean?"

"It means that I believe you're capable of loving more, loving differently, but that I no longer believe myself capable of inspiring a real feeling of love in you."

"No, my friend, you're mistaken. You're more to me than anyone has ever been and more than anyone ever will be. I believe that absolutely. With you I have the great merit of not lying, not pretending to feel what you want me to feel—as you know, many women behave otherwise. Give me credit for that, don't get too excited, try to be reasonable and trust my affection, which is completely and sincerely yours."

Realizing how far apart they were, Mariolle murmured, "What a strange way to think about love—and to talk about it! For you I'm just someone you like to have, more often than not, in the chair beside you. But for me you fill the world. There's no one else in it, I know no one else, I feel no one else is there, and you are all I want."

She had a kind smile for him as she replied, "I know, I can tell, I understand what you're saying. I'm happy to hear what you're saying, and what I say in return is this: Keep on loving me as much as you can, if you can, for that's my greatest happiness; but don't force me to perform a farce which would be painful for me and unworthy of both of us. For some time now, I've sensed this crisis was coming; it's painful for me because I'm so deeply attached to you, but I can't transform my nature and make it like yours. Take me as I am."

Almost before she had finished speaking, he asked, "Have you ever thought, ever believed, just for a day, for even an hour, either before or afterward, that you could love me differently?"

She was unable to reply, thinking for several minutes. He waited in torment, and continued: "You see now, you see that you too dreamed of... something else."

"I may have misjudged my reactions, for a moment," she murmured slowly.

"Oh, that's just psychological quibbling! Hearts can't be analyzed that way."

She thought for a moment, absorbed in her reflections, and added: "Before loving you as I do now, I may have imagined, for a moment, that I would have more... that I would be more excited... but then I would certainly have been less frank, less direct... perhaps less sincere later on."

"Why less sincere, later on?"

"Because you're encasing love in that formula, 'Everything or Nothing,' and to my ears that sounds like 'Everything at first, then Nothing afterward.' It's when the Nothing begins that a woman starts lying."

He answered, very upset now, "But you don't understand my misery and the torment of thinking you could have loved me... differently! You felt as much yourself; so it'll be someone else whom you will love that way."

She answered without hesitation, "I don't think so."

"But why—yes, why? Ever since you've had a notion of love, since you've been touched by the suspicion of this impossible and tormenting hope of mingling your life, your flesh, and your soul with someone else's, of disappearing in him and taking him into yourself, you must have realized the possibility of that ineffable emotion... and one day or another you'll feel it yourself."

"No. It's my imagination that misled me, and was misled about me. I'm giving you all I can give. I've given this a lot of thought since I became your mistress. Please notice that I'm afraid of nothing—not even words. I'm truly quite convinced that I cannot love more or better than I'm doing at this very moment. You can see that I'm talking to you the way I talk to myself. I'm doing this because you're an extremely intelligent man—you understand everything, you can get to the heart of things, and I know that to conceal nothing from you is the best, is the only way to bring us together, and to keep us together for a long time. And that's what I want, my friend."

He listened to her the way a man drinks when he's dying of thirst, and he fell to his knees, his forehead on her skirt. He held both her hands to his lips, murmuring, "Thank you, thank you." When he raised his head to look at her, she had tears in her eyes; then, putting her arms around Mariolle's neck, she drew him to her gently, leaned down, and kissed his eyelids.

"Sit down," she said. "It's not a good idea for you to be kneeling here in front of me."

He sat in a chair, and after a few moments' silence during which they gazed at each other, she asked if he'd take her one of these days to see the Prédolé exhibition people were raving about.

She had a little bronze cupid of Prédolé's that poured water into her bath, and she was eager to visit the Galerie Varin, which was now showing work from his entire career.

They set a date, then Mariolle stood up to go. "Will you be at Auteuil tomorrow?" she asked in almost a whisper.

"Of course I will!" And he left her, dizzy with joy, intoxicated with that "perhaps" which never dies in loving hearts.

6

MADAME de Burne's coupé rolled along the rue de Grenelle as fast as the two horses could trot. The hailstones of a last winter storm, for these were the first days of April, noisily battered the carriage windows and landed on the pavement already speckled with white grains. Pedestrians hurried by under their umbrellas, necks buried in mufflers and overcoat collars. After two weeks of fine weather an untimely cold spell had everyone shivering as if there had been no sign of spring.

Her feet propped against a steaming foot warmer, her body wrapped in a fur whose gentle caress warmed her through her dress, affording a delicious sensation where it touched her bare skin, the young woman was dejectedly thinking that in less than an hour she'd have to take a fiacre to meet André Mariolle at Auteuil. She was strongly tempted to send him a telegram, but over two months ago she had promised herself to do this as rarely as possible, for she had made a tremendous resolution to love him as he loved her. Seeing him suffer so keenly, she had taken pity on him, and after that conversation when she had kissed his eyes in a sincere impulse of sympathy, her feelings for him had actually become, for some time now, warmer and more expansive. She had wondered, surprised by her involuntary coldness, why she shouldn't love him as so many women love their lovers, since she felt deeply attached to him and he pleased her more than all the other men she knew. Such nonchalance in her feelings for him must be due to some lethargy of the heart, which might be overcome like any other lethargy. She made an effort. She tried to rouse herself by thinking about him, to be moved on their days of rendezvous, and sometimes she actually managed to succeed, the way you frighten yourself at night by thinking about ghosts and burglars. She even made an effort, getting a little giddy herself in this game of passion, to be more actively caressing, more aggressive, and at first she succeeded pretty well, driving Mariolle wild with excitement.

So then she thought she was developing an emotion something like the fever that seemed to be consuming him. Her old intermittent dream of love, glimpsed as a possibility that night she decided to give herself to him, somewhat beguiled by the milky mists rising out of the bay of Mont-Saint-Michel, had revived, less seductive, less swathed in clouds of poetry and idealism but more specific, more human, released from illusions after the ordeal of the affair.

And she had sought then, but in vain, those great convulsions that human beings experience, apparently released by the union of two bodies carried away by their souls' emotions. Those convulsions had not occurred.

She persisted, though, simulating arousal, meeting more and more frequently, telling him, "I feel I love you more and more." But she was overcome by fatigue, and it was impossible to deceive herself as well as him any longer. She realized, amazed, that the kisses he covered her with began to irritate her after a while, although she was not entirely indifferent to them. She realized this by the vague lassitude that came over her on the mornings of the days she was supposed to meet him. Why, on those mornings, why didn't she feel, on the contrary, like so many other women, that her flesh was moved by the troubling and longed-for expectation of their lovers' embraces? She accepted them, she endured them tenderly, resigned, then overcome, brutally conquered and quivering despite herself, but never carried away. Could it be that her fine, delicate flesh, so exceptionally aristocratic and refined, harbored unknown shames, shames of a superior and sacred animal, shames still unknown to her modern soul?

Little by little Mariolle understood. He watched her factitious ardor diminish. He divined her devoted ruse, and a deadly and inconsolable disappointment made its way into his soul.

She knew now, as well as he did, that the test had failed and all hope was lost. And this very day, wrapped in her fur, her feet resting on the warmer, shivering comfortably as she watched the hail lash the coupé windows, she no longer had the courage to leave this warmth behind and climb into an icy fiacre to join that poor boy.

Of course the notion of breaking it off, of avoiding his caresses, never occurred to her for a moment. She knew perfectly well that to utterly captivate a man who's in love with you and to keep him for yourself alone, despite countless feminine rivalries, he must be held by the chain that body fastens to body. She knew it because it is fatal, logical, indisputable. It is even loyal to act in accord with this law, and she wanted to remain loyal to him, with all her mistress's probity. So she would give herself again, she would always give herself; but why so often? Wouldn't their actual meetings acquire an added charm for him, a lure of renewal, if they could be spaced out like inestimable and rare felicities conferred by her and which must not be squandered?

On each of her excursions to Auteuil, she had the impression of bestowing upon André the most precious of offerings, an inestimable gift. When one gives in such a fashion, the joy of giving is inseparable from a certain sensation of sacrifice; it is not the intoxication of being taken, it is the pride of being generous and the satisfaction of making another happy.

She even calculated that André's love was more likely to last if she denied herself to him a little more, for every hunger is intensified by fasting, and what is sensual desire but appetite? Once this resolution was made, she decided she would go to Auteuil that very day, but would pretend to be ill. This excursion, which a moment earlier had seemed so painful in such terrible weather, immediately appeared the easiest thing in the world, and she now understood, smiling to herself at this sudden development, why she had so resisted such a normal thing. Just now she hadn't wanted to go—and then she was quite happy to do so. Just now she had resisted because she had reviewed in advance the thousand exasperating little details of the encounter! How she would prick her fingers with the steel pins she always handled so clumsily; how she could never find the clothes she had dropped here and there in the bedroom while hurriedly undressing, already anticipating the hateful task of having to put her things back on *afterward* without a maid.

That prospect made something else occur to her for the first time: Wasn't it rather vulgar, actually quite repugnant in fact, this business of making love on schedule, arranged a day or two ahead of time, like a business appointment or a medical consultation? After a long intimate conversation, what would be more natural than that a kiss should spring to the lips, uniting two mouths which have charmed each other, have actually summoned each other, seduced each other by warm and tender words. But how different that was from a prearranged kiss, booked beforehand, which she would receive once a week, glancing at her watch. Wasn't it even true that she had occasionally felt a vague impulse, on days when she wasn't *scheduled* to meet André, to join him *impromptu*, while such impulses rarely occurred to her when she went to him with the precautions of a house thief, in a dirty fiacre, her heart distracted by all these *arrangements*?

Oh, the time for Auteuil! She had calculated it on the clocks of all her friends; she had seen it approaching, minute by minute, at the Baroness de Frémines's, at the Marquise de Bratiane's, at pretty Madame Le Prieur's, when she would spend her afternoons traipsing around Paris in order not to be at home, where an unexpected visit or some unforeseen obstacle might have kept her a prisoner of her own life.

Suddenly she decided. "All right, a day off: I'll go late and avoid bothering him too much." So then she slid open a secret panel hidden in the black silk lining of her coupé, revealing a sort of boudoir. Once the two tiny doors of this hiding place were folded back, a hinged mirror appeared which she raised level with her face. Behind the mirror, lined up in satin niches, were several little silver objects: a box for rice powder, a lip pencil, two scent bottles, an inkwell, a penholder, scissors, a tiny paper knife for cutting the latest novel, which one might want to read en route. An exquisite clock the size and shape of a round gold walnut was set in the silk: the hands indicated four o'clock.

Madame de Burne was thinking, "I still have at least an hour," and she touched a spring, which signaled the footman sitting beside the coachman to pick up the speaking tube. She pulled out the other end, concealed in the black silk lining, and bringing her lips to the tiny rock-crystal mouthpiece, she ordered, "To the Austrian embassy."

Then she looked in the mirror. She looked at herself as she always did, with the contentment one feels in the person one loves best in all the world, then slipped off her fur robe to arrange her dress, a late-winter confection, its collar trimmed with a row of fine white feathers, gleaming in the darkness of the coupé; they spread over her shoulders, shading to a light gray, as if on a wing. Her waist too was bordered with this same downy decoration, which gave the young woman the curious look of a wild bird. On her hat, a sort of toque, there were more feathers, an aigrette of brighter colors, and her lovely blond head seemed ready to fly off with the teals, through the swirling hail into the gray skies beyond.

She was still studying her reflection when the carriage turned sharply under the great gates of the embassy. Then she pulled the fur around her once more, lowered the mirror, closed the tiny doors of the panel, and when the coupé had come to a halt, said to her coachman, "Return to the house; I won't be needing you any more."

And then she asked the footman who came out on the embassy steps, "Is the princess at home?"

"Yes, madame."

She went in, climbed the stairs, and made her way to the little salon where Princess von Malten was writing letters. Recognizing her friend, the ambassadress stood up with an expression of great pleasure, her eyes shining, and the women kissed each other on both cheeks, just at the corner of the lips. Then they sat down together on two little chairs in front of the fire. It was evident how fond they were of each other, how delighted to be together, how well they understood each other on every point, for they were very much alike, of the same female type, raised in the same atmosphere, endowed with the same sensations, though Princess von Malten was a Swede married to an Austrian. These two women exerted a mysterious and singular attraction upon each other, which produced a sincere feeling of well-being and profound contentment when they were together. Their chatter would continue without interruption for half a day at a time, trivial and fascinating to them both, delighting as they did in the revelation of the same tastes.

"Now you see how much I love you!" Madame de Burne exclaimed. "You're coming to me for dinner tonight, and even so I couldn't resist stopping by to see you. It's a passion, my dear."

"One I share," the princess answered with a smile, and by a kind of professional habit, they complimented each other, coquettish as if facing a suitor, but flirting differently, engaged in another kind of struggle, no longer with an adversary but a rival.

Chattering away, Madame de Burne glanced now and then at the clock. It was nearly five. He had been waiting an hour for her. "Long enough," she decided, and rose to go.

"Already?" the princess protested.

"Oh yes, I've got to rush. Someone's waiting for me," her friend answered boldly. "I'd much rather stay with you." They exchanged kisses once more, and having asked for a fiacre to be called, Madame de Burne left the embassy.

The horse had a limp and dragged the old carriage with great difficulty. The young woman felt the animal's exhaustion as if it were her own. Like the winded creature, she found the distance a trial and the effort to cover it painful. Gradually the pleasure of seeing André consoled her, but the thought of what she was about to do made her anxious.

She found him standing half frozen behind the door. Sudden gusts made the treetops thrash, and hailstones hammered on their umbrella as they hurried through the garden and into the pavilion. Their feet sank in the mire. How melancholy the garden looked, denuded and muddy. André was pale and seemed to be suffering. "Lord, how cold it is," she said, once they were inside. Yet huge fires were blazing in both rooms, though they had been lit only since noon, and the damp still clung to the walls; she shivered, adding: "I think I won't take off my fur just yet." She opened only the top clasps of her wrap, and in her feathered gown she looked even more like one of those migratory birds that never alight anywhere for long. He sat down beside her. "Tonight," she announced, "I'm giving a charming dinner party I'm so looking forward to."

"Who's invited?"

"You, first of all, of course; and then Prédolé, whom I'm quite eager to know."

"You're having Prédolé?"

"Yes, Lamarthe is bringing him."

"What an odd man for you to be having to dinner. As a rule sculptors aren't likely to appeal to women like you, and this one less than all the others."

"Oh dear! Well, I can't help it. I admire him so much!"

For the last two months, since his exhibition at the Galerie Varin, the sculptor Prédolé had been the darling of Paris. He had been praised already, and his prices had risen accordingly; people said of him, "He makes the loveliest little women!" But when the artistic public, the people who regarded themselves as true connoisseurs, was invited to judge his entire output gathered in the galleries of the rue Varin, there had been an explosion of enthusiasm. Here was the revelation of an unexpected charm, the discovery of a unique gift for expressing elegance and grace! It was as if they were present at the birth of a new seduction of the human form.

The artist had made a specialty of small statues, lightly—very lightly—clad, their delicate modeling expressed with an unimaginable perfection. His dancers in particular, of which he exhibited countless pen-and-ink studies along with the sculptures, revealed in their gestures, their poses, and by the harmony of their attitudes and movements all the rare and supple beauty the female body could propose.

For a month now Madame de Burne had made numerous efforts to invite Prédolé to her house. But the sculptor was shy, even something of a boor, people said. Finally she had succeeded in luring him to the rue du Général Foy through the good offices of Lamarthe, who had made frantic and sincere appeals to the grateful sculptor.

"Who else is coming?" Mariolle asked.

"Princess von Malten."

That annoyed him: the woman was preposterous. "And besides her?"

"Massival, Bernhaus, and Georges de Maltry. No one else—the inner circle, actually. Have you ever met Prédolé?"

"Yes, here and there."

"What's he like?"

"Remarkable. He's the only man I know who's completely in love with his art, and actually most interesting when you can get him to talk about it."

She was delighted, and repeated, "It really will be charming."

He had taken her hand under the fur. He pressed it gently, then kissed it. That was when she suddenly realized she had forgotten to say she was feeling ill, and casting about for some other reason, she murmured, "Lord, it's still so cold!"

"Do you think so?"

"I'm chilled to the bone."

He stood up to look at the thermometer: the mercury was indeed quite low. Then he sat down again beside her. She had just said "Lord, it's still so cold!" and he thought he knew why. For three weeks he had noticed at each of their meetings the unfailing diminution of her attempts at affection. He guessed that she was sufficiently tired of this pretense to be unable to go on with it, and he himself was so exasperated by her inability to love him, so tormented by his raging, futile desire for this woman, that in his hours of despairing solitude he had begun to tell himself, "Better to break it off than to go on like this."

He asked her now, to be sure he understood her intentions more clearly, "You're not taking off your fur this afternoon?"

"Oh, I'd better not," she said, "I've been coughing a little all morning. This awful weather has given me a sore throat. I don't want to get really ill." And after a silence: "If I hadn't wanted so see you so much, I wouldn't have come." Since he made no response, lacerated as he was with disappointment and tense with rage, she continued: "After the lovely days of these last two weeks, this cold spell is very dangerous." She looked out at the garden, where the trees were already showing some green under the melting snow that dripped from the branches.

He gazed at her, and thought, "That's how much she loves me!" For the first time, a sort of hatred possessed him, the hatred of a defeated man for this woman's face, for her impenetrable soul, and for her adorable body, so pursued and so elusive.

"She claims she's cold," he said to himself. "She's only cold because I'm here. If there were a party somewhere, one of those idiotic affairs which satisfy the entire existence of these trivial creatures, she'd brave everything, she'd risk her life to be there. If she could show off her dresses by doing so, she'd ride in an open carriage on the coldest day of the year! They're all like that nowadays." He gazed at her where she sat, facing him so calmly, and he knew that there was only one desire in that adorable little forehead, the desire not to go on with this tête-à-tête which was becoming too painful.

Was it true that there had ever existed, that there existed still, women capable of passion, women shaken by emotion, women who suffer, who weep, who frenziedly abandon themselves, who embrace and cling and moan, women who love with their flesh as much as with their soul, with lips that speak and eyes that gaze, with hearts that beat and hands that caress, women who brave the world for the sake of love, women quivering with passion and with happiness who seek by day and by darkness, guarded and threatened, intrepid and trembling, the lover who will take them in his arms...

Horrible, this love to which he was now chained, a love without purpose and without aim, without joy and without triumph, a love that sickened, weakened, laid waste to everything, a love without sweetness and without intoxication, breeding nothing but regret and foreboding, tears and pain, hinting at the ecstasy of shared caresses only by some intolerable longing for kisses not to be wakened on cold lips, sterile and dry as dead leaves.

He gazed at her, so charmingly imprisoned in that feathered confection. Were not such gowns the real enemies to be vanquished, even more than the women of whom they were the jealous guardians? How he resented these precious, coquettish barriers which jailed and defended his mistress against him! "Your gown is lovely," he said, unable to speak of what was tormenting him.

She answered, with a smile, "Wait till you see what I'll be wearing tonight." Then she coughed several times, and managed to speak through her effort. "I'm really catching cold here. Let me go, my friend. The sun will shine soon again, and I shall do the same."

He did not protest, disheartened and realizing that no effort could vanquish the inertia of this passionless creature, that it was over, all over, that there was no hope now for fervent words to be stammered by those tranquil lips, for the light of love to flash from those calm eyes. And suddenly he felt rising within him a violent resolve to escape this tormenting domination. She had nailed him to a cross on which he bled from every limb, and watched him agonize with no comprehension of his sufferings, though she was pleased to have inflicted them. But he would wrest himself free of this instrument of torture, leaving on it pieces of his body, shreds of his flesh, and all of his lacerated heart. Like some wild beast that hunters have nearly killed, he would escape, would find some solitary hiding place where his wounds might heal until he felt only the dull aches the mutilated endure until death.

"Goodbye then," he said to her.

Moved by the sadness in his voice, she reminded him: "Till this evening, my friend."

And he repeated: "Till this evening…Goodbye." Then he accompanied her to the door of the garden, and came back and sat down, alone, in front of the fire.

Alone! And it really was cold, even in front of the fire. It was all over. How sad that was. All over. What a horrible thought! No more hoping, no more waiting, no more dreaming of her with that glow in his heart which keeps us alive on this grim earth, like bonfires lit on dark nights. No more nights of solitary emotion when almost till dawn he walked back and forth in his bedroom, thinking of her; and then those awakenings when he'd tell himself as he opened his eyes, "Soon I'll be seeing her in our little house."

How he loved her! How he loved her and how hard it would be, how long it would take to cure himself of that! She had gone because it was cold! He could still see her as she had been just now, gazing at him, bewitching him the better to break his heart! Better! It was pretty well broken already, he could feel the crack: it was already an old wound, one she had opened and then bandaged time and again, and now she had made an incurable mess of it with the knife of her mortal indifference. He could feel that something was leaking out of that broken heart of his, something filling his body, it was up to his throat now, he was choking on it. Then, putting his hands over his eyes as if to hide this weakness from himself, he began to cry. She had left because it was cold! He would have walked naked through the snow to be with her, anywhere he could find her. He would have thrown himself off the roof if he could land at her feet. He remembered an old story—it had become a legend—about the Hill of Two Lovers that you passed on your way to Rouen: a young girl who obeyed her father's cruel whim forbidding her to marry her lover unless she carried him up the hill, dragging him there on her hands and knees, and dying when she reached the top. Love is nothing now except a legend, to be sung in ballads or read in silly novels.

Hadn't his mistress herself, in one of their first conversations, made a remark he had never forgotten: "Nowadays men and women don't love each other to the point of really doing themselves any harm. Believe me, I know both sides of the matter." She was wrong about him, but not about herself, for she had gone on to say, "In any case, I warn you that I'm quite incapable of really loving anyone..."

Anyone? Could that be true? She didn't care for him, no. He was sure of that now, but could she care for someone else? Not for him?... She couldn't love him. Why was that? And then the sensation of having missed everything life had to offer overwhelmed him as it had so often in the past. He had accomplished nothing, achieved nothing, succeeded in nothing. Tempted by all the arts, he had lacked the courage to dedicate himself completely to any of them, and the perseverance to gain any real mastery. He had been rewarded by no triumph, no exalted taste had ennobled his character. His one sincere effort to conquer a woman's heart had failed like all the rest. It couldn't be denied: he was nothing but a failure.

He was still crying; the tears ran between his fingers and slid down his face, moistening his mustache; he could taste the salt on his lips. That bitterness added to his misery and his despair.

When he raised his head, he saw that it was night. There was just time to go home and dress for dinner at Madame de Burne's.

7

ANDRÉ MARIOLLE was the first to arrive at Madame Michèle de Burne's. He sat down and gazed around him at the walls, the tapestries, the furniture, and the bibelots, the familiar interior he loved because it was hers, where he had come to know her and where he had learned to love her, where he had discovered in himself and felt growing day by day this passion of his, until the moment of its futile victory. How ardently he had waited for her to appear in this charming room expressly created as an appropriate setting for its exquisite inhabitant. How familiar to him its iris scent, so simple and so distinguished, had become. Here he had indulged so many expectations, nursed so many hopes, explored so many emotions, and finally suffered so many defeats. He pressed the arms of the easy chair in which he had so often sat like the hands of a departing friend, and gazed at her as she smiled and talked to him. He almost wished that she would not come now, that no one would come, that he could stay here alone the whole night, dreaming of his love as one keeps a vigil for the dead. Then he would leave at dawn for a long absence, perhaps for good.

The door opened. She appeared and came to him, hands outstretched. He controlled himself, betraying nothing. This was not a woman but a living bouquet, an unimaginable bouquet: a garland of pinks encircled her waist and cascaded over her skirt to her feet; another garland of forget-me-nots and lilies of the valley wreathed her bare arms and shoulders, while three fantastic orchids seemed to spring from her throat to caress the pale flesh of her breasts with their own pink-and-carmine flesh of magical blooms. Her blond hair was strewn with enamel violets among which glistened tiny diamonds, and still others quivered on gold pins, sparkling like drops of water in the perfumed folds of her gown.

"I know I'll have a migraine, but I don't care—the flowers suit me, don't you think?" Her perfume was like a spring garden, and she looked fresher than her garlands. Mariolle gazed at her, transfixed, thinking it would be as barbaric to take this woman in his arms at this moment as to trample on a flower bed in full bloom. Bodies, arrayed like this, were no more than a pretext for adornment—no longer an object to be loved. They looked like flowers, like birds, like anything else in the world as much as women. Their mothers, women of past generations, had employed their arts of coquetry to enhance their beauty, but primarily they sought to please by the seductiveness of their bodies, by the power of their natural grace, by the irresistible attraction a woman's form exerts on the hearts of men. Nowadays coquetry was everything, artifice had become not only the means but the end as well, for women made use of it to irritate their rivals and excite a sterile envy as much as to conquer the men's hearts. For whom, then, was this extraordinary creation intended? For him, for the lover, or to humiliate the Princess von Malten?

The door opened, the princess was announced, and Madame de Burne sprang toward her. Carefully shielding the orchids, she embraced her friend, lips parted, with a little pout of affection. It was a pretty and most desirable kiss, fervently given and received by both mouths. Mariolle gave a start of anguish. Not once had she ever run toward him with such happy impetuosity; and like a whiplash the thought roused his mind to fury: "Such women are no longer made for us."

Massival appeared, and behind him Monsieur de Pradon, Count de Bernhaus, and Georges de Maltry, resplendent with English chic. Only Lamarthe and Prédolé were still to come. Someone mentioned the sculptor, and every voice was raised in his praise. He had resuscitated grace, recovered the tradition of the Renaissance with something more—modern sincerity; he was, according to Georges de Maltry, the exquisite exponent of a lissome humanity. These phrases, and others of the same sort, had for the last two months echoed in every salon in Paris, given out by every mouth, received by all ears.

At last the man himself appeared, to general astonishment: a heavyset fellow of indeterminate age, with the shoulders of a peasant and a masterful head covered with a grayish stubble; a powerful nose, fleshy lips, and a timid, embarrassed expression. He held his arms away from his body with a clumsiness doubtless attributable to the huge hands which stuck out of his sleeves. They were broad and thick, with hairy, muscular fingers—hands of Hercules or a butcher, awkward, embarrassed at being seen yet impossible to hide. This face, though, was illuminated by the clearest pair of eyes, gray, piercing, and of an extraordinary vivacity; they alone seemed alive in this whole stolid creature, staring, scrutinizing, searching, casting quick, mobile flashes in all directions. No one could be unaware of the powerful, vital intelligence animating such penetrating glances.

Madame de Burne, a little disappointed, politely indicated a chair, and the sculptor sat down. And there he remained, apparently ill at ease in such company, in such surroundings.

Lamarthe, attempting to break the ice, went over to his friend. "My dear fellow," he said, "I want to show you where you are. You've just met our divine hostess; now have a look at what surrounds her." He pointed to the Houdon bust on the mantel; and then, on a Boule desk, Clodion's figures of two women dancing together, and finally, on a corner shelf, four choice Tanagra figurines.

Prédolé's face suddenly brightened as if he had found his children who had been lost in the desert. He stood up and walked toward the four little earthenware figures, and when he seized two of them in those formidable hands apparently made for slaughtering oxen, Madame de Burne trembled for her treasures. But as soon as he touched them, he appeared to be caressing them, for he handled them with surprising delicacy, slowly turning them between thick fingers that had become as agile as any juggler's. Seeing him contemplate and finger them this way, everyone in the room felt that this ungainly creature had a unique tenderness in his soul and hands, an ideal delicacy for fondling anything small and elegant.

"Lovely, aren't they?" Lamarthe asked. And then the sculptor praised them as if he had known them for years, and spoke a little about other remarkable examples of this antique art, his voice low but calm and secure in the service of a mind familiar with the value of the terms employed.

Guided by the novelist, Prédolé inspected the other fine bibelots Madame de Burne had collected on her friends' advice. He recognized them with delight and some surprise to find them in such a place, constantly picking the objects up and slowly turning them around, as if to put himself in tender contact with each one. One bronze statuette, heavy as a cannonball, was hidden in a dark corner; the sculptor picked it up in one hand, brought it over to a lamp, admired it for a long moment, then put it back without any apparent effort.

"There's a man made for the struggle with marble and stone!" Lamarthe remarked. And everyone looked at the sculptor with feeling.

A servant came in and announced, "Madame is served." The mistress of the house took Prédolé's arm to walk into the dining room, and when she had seated him on her right, she asked him with great courtesy, as she might have questioned the scion of some illustrious family about the precise origin of his name, "Your art, monsieur, has the further merit of being the oldest art of all, is that not so?"

He answered in his calm tone of voice, "Good Lord, madame, the biblical shepherds played their flutes—so music is probably older, though for most of us real music does not date back so far. But true sculpture does—very far."

"And do you care for music as well?" she asked.

"Madame, I love all the arts," he answered with grave conviction.

"Who would you say is the founder of yours?" she asked again.

He thought for a moment, and with a sweetness in his voice as if he were telling a touching personal anecdote, replied, "According to the Greek tradition, it was Daedalus the Athenian; but a more appealing legend attributes this discovery to a potter from Sicyon named Dibutades. When his daughter Kora had drawn a line around the shadow of her beloved's profile on the wall behind him, her father filled this silhouette with clay and modeled it into a bust. My art was born!"

Lamarthe murmured, "Delightful." Then, after a silence, he continued. "Now, if only you would oblige us, Prédolé!" And turning to Madame de Burne: "You cannot imagine, madame, how interesting this man is when he talks about what he loves— how he manages to describe it, to make it real for others to love as well." But the sculptor did not seem inclined to pose or perorate; he had tucked a corner of his napkin into his shirt collar so as not to stain his waistcoat and noisily continued eating with a peasant's respect for his soup. Then he drank a glass of wine and sat up, looking more at ease in this company. Occasionally he tried to turn around, for he had noticed, reflected in a mirror, a modern group of sculptures behind him, on the mantel. He did not recognize the work, but tried to guess the creator. After some moments, impatient to find out if he had judged correctly, he asked, "That's by Falguières, isn't it?"

Madame de Burne burst out laughing. "Yes, it is. How could you find that out, just by looking in a mirror?"

Prédolé smiled in his turn. "Ah, madame, I can always tell the sculpture of someone who also paints, just as I can recognize the painting of someone who also makes sculpture. It's not in the least like the work of someone who practices just one art."

Wanting his friend to shine, Lamarthe requested explanations, and Prédolé obliged. Speaking slowly and carefully, he characterized and defined the painting of sculptors and the sculpture of painters in so clear, original, and novel a manner that the guests listened to him with their eyes as well as their ears.

He went on to the history of art, choosing examples from period after period, as far back as the first Italian masters, who were both painters and sculptors, Nicola and Giovanni Pisano, Donatello, Lorenzo Ghiberti. He quoted Diderot's curious opinions on the same subject, and ended with Ghiberti's baptistery doors, so vivid and dramatic that they seemed more like painted canvases than bas-reliefs. His heavy hands working in front of him as if they were full of soft clay, and as they moved becoming flexible and light enough to dazzle the onlookers, he reconstructed the work he was describing with such conviction that his listeners followed his fingers as they raised above the plates and glasses every image his tongue expressed. Then, presented with some of his favorite dishes, he fell silent and began to eat. After that, until the end of the meal, he spoke little, barely following the conversation which veered from theater gossip to political rumors, from balls to weddings, from an article in *La Revue des Deux Mondes* to a newly opened racetrack. He ate a good deal and drank moderately without seeming to be affected by it, his ideas remaining clear and his thinking consistent and unexcited by the good wine.

When the company returned to the salon, Lamarthe, who had not obtained all he had hoped for from the sculptor, drew him to a glass display case to show him a priceless object, a silver inkstand cast and engraved by Benvenuto Cellini. Prédolé was seized by a sort of rapture; he contemplated the treasure like a beloved mistress's face, and overcome by enthusiasm, released a stream of ideas about Cellini's work, ideas as graceful and sensitive as the art of the great sculptor himself; and then, realizing that the company was hanging on his words, he let himself go and, seated in a large armchair, holding and gazing steadily at the inkstand which had just been put into his hands, he related his impressions of all the masterpieces of the art known to him, revealing every aspect of his sensibility and articulating the strange intoxication which the grace of forms communicated to his soul through his eyes.

For ten years he had scoured the world for nothing but marble, stone, bronze, and wood carved by inspired hands, or else for gold and silver, ivory and brass, substances transformed into masterpieces by the fingers of masters. And he himself seemed to carve as he spoke, producing wondrous reliefs and delicious surfaces by means of the precision of his words.

The men standing around him listened closely, while the two women, sitting near the fire, seemed a trifle bored and whispered to each other from time to time, perplexed that so much delight could be taken from the mere contours of objects. When Prédolé fell silent, Lamarthe, enthralled and gratified, shook his hand and said in a voice filled with the emotion of a shared passion, "Really, my friend, I feel the only proper response is to embrace you. You are the one inspired artist of our moment, the only one who truly loves what he creates, who finds his happiness there, and is never satiated or fatigued. It is the spirit of art in its purest form in which you work. By the inflection of a line you produce the beautiful, and you care for nothing else on earth. I drink this glass of eau-de-vie to your health, monsieur."

Then the conversation became general once more, though tentative and a little abashed by the ideas that had filled the air of that pretty salon furnished with so many precious objects. Prédolé left early, explaining that he began work at dawn every morning. When he had gone, Lamarthe, still in a daze of enthusiasm, asked Madame de Burne, "Well, what did you make of our master?"

She answered a little hesitantly, her expression petulant and slightly dismissive, "Interesting, quite. But rather long-winded, wouldn't you say?"

The novelist smiled, thinking, "Of course, he didn't admire your gown, and you yourself are the only one of your bibelots he failed to notice." After a few flattering remarks he went over to where Princess von Malten was sitting, to pay court where it was certainly due. Count de Bernhaus approached the mistress of the house, seeming to collapse at her feet on a little stool. Mariolle,

Massival, Maltry, and Monsieur de Pradon continued discussing the sculptor, who had made a powerful impression on them all. Monsieur de Maltry was likening him to the old masters, whose entire lives were embellished and illuminated by the exclusive and devouring love of beauty in all its manifestations, elaborating the subject with subtle turns of phrase at once telling and tedious.

Massival, tired of listening to observations about an art not his own, went over to the princess, standing beside Lamarthe who soon yielded his seat in order to rejoin the men. "Shall we leave soon?" he asked Mariolle.

"Yes, I think it's time."

The novelist enjoyed nocturnal conversations, or rather monologues, that echoed in the empty streets as he walked a fellow guest home. His sharp, strident voice seemed to cling to the walls of the houses they passed. These were his moments of greatest eloquence and perspicacity, when he felt at his wittiest and most original. Such outpourings usually afforded him just the kind of attention he required, and he was preparing for a good night's rest after this modest exertion of legs and lungs.

As for Mariolle, he was at the end of his strength. All of his wretchedness and misfortune, all of his grievances and his irremediable disappointment had been seething inside him ever since he had crossed Madame de Burne's threshold. He couldn't bear the place another minute and was determined to leave and never return. When he had said good night to his hostess, she had returned his thanks with a distracted smile.

The two men walked down the street together. The wind had dropped, and the air was warmer than it had been all day. It was mild as it can be only after a spring hailstorm, and the sky was filled with stars which twinkled as if, in that immense space, a breath of summer had restored them to life. The sidewalks had become gray and dry again, while in the roadway, puddles still gleamed under the gaslight.

Lamarthe said, "That Prédolé is a happy man!... He loves one thing, his art: that's all he can think about, all he lives for, and it consoles him, delights him, makes his entire existence happy and good. He really is a great artist of the old school. And he certainly doesn't bother about women, our kind of women at any rate, with their baubles and laces and the rest of their disguises. Did you notice how little attention he paid to our two pretty ladies, who certainly were attractive tonight, weren't they? The only thing that appeals to him is line and form, the pure plasticity of the figure, nothing artificial. I suppose it was inevitable that our lovely hostess would find him unendurable and idiotic. For her a Houdon bust and four Tanagra statuettes or a Cellini inkstand are merely little embellishments appropriate to the rich natural setting of a masterpiece like herself: herself and her gown, for her gown is certainly part of herself; it's the new note she's sounding nightly for her beauty. How frivolous a woman like that is, and how...how selfish!"

He broke off, tapping the sidewalk with his cane so sharply that the sound echoed down the street for several seconds. Then he continued. "A woman like that knows, understands, and enjoys what makes her effective: the gown and the jewels which change fashion every ten years. But when it comes to anything that requires delicate artistic penetration and a disinterested, purely aesthetic exercise of the senses, she hasn't a clue. These ladies, moreover, have quite rudimentary senses, have you noticed? Female senses, which cannot be trained and are inaccessible to what doesn't immediately appeal to female egotism, which absorbs everything in their lives. Their subtlety is that of a savage, a warrior, a hunter—the subtlety of combat and trapping...Most women are incapable of enjoying material pleasures of a lesser order, the kind which require physical training and a refined attention to some particular organ, like the palate. When they happen, by some miracle, to respect the art of cooking, they stop there and lack all appreciation for a fine wine, which appeals only to male palates—a good wine actually speaks!"

He gave another tap of his cane to underline his last insight and add a period to his sentence. Then he continued. "Of course we mustn't expect too much of them. But that lack of taste and comprehension that darkens their intellectual understanding of higher things frequently blinds them even more where we're concerned. It's no use at all, when it comes to attracting, not to mention seducing them, to have a soul, a heart, a brain—exceptional qualities and virtues, as in the old days, when a man might be loved for his courage, his conscience, his valor. Our ladies today are performance artists, the strolling players of love, dashing off what they've been handed by a tradition they no longer believe in. They need matinee idols to feed them their cues, and play their parts just as badly as our ladies..."

They walked beside each other in silence for a few moments. Mariolle had listened attentively, mentally repeating each phrase, silently approving his friend's verdict from the depths of his grieving heart. He knew, moreover, that a sort of Italian adventurer, Prince Epilati, had appeared in Paris to give fencing lessons, his elegance and his supple vigor much in demand in certain aristocratic circles and much on display in elite *salles d'armes*, wearing skin-tight black silk outfits and lately monopolizing the attention and the coquetry of little Baroness de Frémines. As Lamarthe walked on in silence, Mariolle observed, "Well, it's our fault; we choose badly. There must be other kinds of women."

To which the novelist replied, "The only ones still capable of attachment are shopgirls or sentimental little bourgeoises, impecunious and unhappily married. I've had occasion to afford succor to one or another of these souls in distress. They're overflowing with sentiment, as I just said, but the sentiment is so vulgar that the exchange for our version is a very bad bargain. What I say is this: that among our wealthy young people, where the women have no real desire and no real need, so that all they want is to be amused without incurring any danger, and where the men have regulated their pleasure exactly to the same degree that they've organized whatever work they do—I say that the good old natural powers of attraction which used to draw the sexes together have disappeared!"

To which Mariolle murmured in reply, "You're quite right."

His longing to get away increased—to get away from these people, these puppets who because they had nothing better to do mimicked the lovely old ways of a life of passion and no longer enjoyed one drop of its lost sweetness. "Good night," he said, "I'm going home to bed."

He went home, sat down at his desk, and wrote:

Farewell, madame. Do you remember my first letter? I said farewell to you then, but I didn't go. What a mistake I made! By the time you receive these words I shall have left Paris. Need I explain why? Men like me should never meet women like you. If I were an artist and my emotions could be expressed so as to afford me some relief, you might have inspired me with some talent; but I am only a poor fellow who has incurred, along with my love for you, a cruel and unbearable distress. When I first encountered you, I should not have believed myself capable of feeling and suffering in this fashion. Another woman, in your place, would have poured into my heart a divine happiness even as she enthralled it. But you have merely tortured it. I know you can't help it; I reproach you for nothing, and I bear you no ill will. Indeed I have no right to address these lines to you. Forgive me. You are so constituted that you cannot feel as I do, nor can you even guess what happens to me when I come to see you, when you speak to me, and when I contemplate you. Yes, you consent, you accept me, and you even offer me a calm and reasonable happiness for which I should thank you on my knees for the rest of my life. But I do not want it. Ah, what a dreadful, tormenting love it is which constantly seeks the charity of a warm phrase or of a fervent caress, and which never receives any such thing! My heart is as empty as the belly of the beggar who has run after you a long while, hand outstretched. You have tossed him lovely things, but not bread. It is bread, it is love I needed. I leave you wretched and poor, famished for your tenderness, a few crumbs of which would have saved me. Now all I have in the world is a cruel memory which must be obliterated. Which is what I shall attempt to achieve.

Farewell, madame. Forgive me, thank you, forgive me. This very evening, I love you with all my heart and soul. Adieu.

André Mariolle

PART THREE

I

A RADIANT morning was gilding all Paris. Mariolle climbed into the carriage waiting at his door, a suitcase and two trunks in the luggage rack. The night before he had made his valet pack enough clothes and everything else for a long absence, leaving as his temporary address: "Fontainebleau, poste restante. He brought no one with him, determined not to see a face which would remind him of Paris, nor to hear a voice that would be familiar when he thought of certain things.

"Gare de Lyon," he shouted to the driver, and the fiacre started on its way. That was when he thought of that other departure for Mont-Saint-Michel, last spring. In three months it would be a year since then. To empty his mind of such things, he stared out into the street.

The fiacre turned into the avenue des Champs-Élysées sparkling under a shower of spring sunlight. The green leaves, released already by the warmth of the last few weeks and scarcely impeded by the last two days of hail and cold rain, seemed to diffuse, so quickly did they open on this luminous morning, an odor of cool verdure and evaporating sap among the already spreading branches. It was one of those mornings of budding life when in the public gardens and along the avenues you could feel that in a day or two the horse chestnuts would blossom all over Paris, like so many chandeliers being lit at once. Earth's life was awakening to another summer, and the tarry pavement seemed to quiver faintly, stirred by the roots underneath. Shaken by the jolting fiacre, Mariolle was thinking, "At last I'll have some peace, watching the forest come to life in the spring." The train trip seemed long to him, stiff as he was after those sleepless hours of self-pity, as if he had spent ten nights at a dying man's bedside. Getting off in Fontainebleau, he visited the first notary he could find to inquire about renting a furnished chalet on the forest's edge. Several were recommended; the one whose photograph pleased him most had just been vacated by a young couple who had spent the whole winter in the village of Montigny-sur-Loing. The notary, for all his gravity, managed a sidelong smile, apparently suspecting a love affair.

"You're alone, monsieur?"

"Yes, I'm alone."

"No servants, even?"

"No servants, even. I left mine in Paris. I'll find someone in the neighborhood to take care of me. I'm here to work in complete isolation."

"You'll have it, this time of year."

And a few minutes later, Mariolle and his trunks were in an open landau on the way to Montigny. The forest was awakening. Beneath the great trees, their limbs already covered with a faint shadow of foliage, the underbrush was burgeoning. The silvery limbs of the hasty birches seemed already dressed for summer, while the huge oaks showed, at the tips of their branches, the faintest green patches. The beeches, having opened their pointed buds, had shed the last dead leaves of the year before. The grass along the road, not yet covered by impenetrable shade, grew thick and shiny, lacquered with new juices, and this scent of fresh growth, which Mariolle had already smelled in the avenue des Champs-Élysées, now enveloped him until he was immersed in a huge bath of vegetal life germinating in the first days of sunshine. He took deep breaths, like a man released from jail, and as if he had just broken his bonds, he gently stretched out his arms on either side of the landau, letting his hands dangle over the two wheels.

It was good to breathe an air so fresh, so pure, yet he would have to inhale it a long, long time to be revived enough to suffer a little less, to feel that cool breath taken through his lungs at last and sliding over the open wound of his heart, actually healing it!

He passed Marlotte, where the driver pointed out the Hôtel Corot, which had just opened and whose originality was much talked about. Then they took a road between the forest on the left and, on the right, a broad plain dotted with groves of trees and extending to a hilly horizon. After that they rolled down a long village street, blinding white between two interminable rows of little tile-roofed houses. Here and there, an enormous lilac bush in full bloom reared up over the spotless walls.

This road followed a narrow valley descending to a small river. This rapid, noisy, winding stream, which on one bank washed the foundations of the village houses and their garden walls, on the other watered meadows where young saplings unfurled their frail, hardly open foliage.

Mariolle easily found the house the notary had indicated, and it delighted him, for it was an old dwelling restored by a painter who had spent five years there before tiring of it and putting it up for rent. The house was very near the river, separated from it by a fine garden which ended in a terrace bordered by lindens. The Loing, pouring over a dam a couple of feet high, flowed past the terrace in great circular eddies. On the other side of the house the windows overlooked meadows.

"I can be cured here," Mariolle decided. In the event the house proved satisfactory, he had arranged matters with the notary; the driver took his answer, and now he must deal with moving in, which went quickly enough, the mayor's secretary having sent two village women, one to cook, the other to clean the rooms and do the laundry. On the ground floor was a living room, a dining room, the kitchen, and two other small rooms; upstairs, a handsome bedroom and a sort of study which the painter had used as his studio. All this was nicely furnished, evidently by someone who had fallen in love with both the house and its setting.

It was a little frowsy now, with the sullen look of a place that had been moved out of. Yet it was clear that the little house had been inhabited quite recently. A sweet scent still floated on the air of every room. Mariolle recognized it: "That's verbena. The woman who lived here before me had simple tastes...Lucky man!"

Evening was approaching: all these matters had taken up most of the day. He sat down in front of an open window, drinking in the sweet moist fragrance of the damp grass and watching the setting sun send long shadows across the meadows.

The faint voices of the two servants gossiping as they prepared his dinner came up the staircase, while through the windows entered the lowing of cows, the barking of dogs, and the calls of men driving the cattle home or talking to friends across the river. It was truly peaceful here. Mariolle wondered for the thousandth time since that morning: "What did she think when she got my letter? What will she do?" Then he asked himself, "What's she doing at this very moment?" He looked at his watch—six thirty. "She's home now, she's receiving company." He could see the salon, and he imagined her talking with Princess von Malten, Baroness de Frémines, Massival, and Count de Bernhaus. Suddenly he was shaken by a fit of rage. He wanted to be there. This was the time he usually came to her house, and he felt a certain uneasiness—not regret, for his will was firm, but a sort of physical suffering like that of a patient denied his usual dose of morphine.

He no longer saw the meadows, nor the sun disappearing behind the hills on the horizon. He saw only her among her friends, devoured by those worldly preoccupations which had stolen her from him. "Don't think about it anymore," he told himself, or did he say it aloud? He stood up, went down to the garden, walked to the terrace. Mist rose off the river, and the sensation of cool dampness, chilling his sad heart, sent him back inside. His place was set at the table in the dining room. He ate what was put before him and then, having nothing to do, feeling in his body and in his soul that growing malaise which had come over him just now, he lay down on his bed and closed his eyes—yes, he would sleep awhile. But to no purpose. With every thought he saw and suffered from the image of that woman.

Who would be the favorite now? Most likely Count de Bernhaus. Just the man for this creature display, the man so much in public view, so elegant, so sought after, and evidently pleasing to her, for to conquer him she had employed all her weapons, even though she had been the mistress of another man at the time...

Under the mastery of these gnawing thoughts, his soul grew sluggish, diverted into somnolent maunderings in which the pair continually reappeared, that man, her, her, that man... Real sleep never came, and all night he saw them gliding around him, provoking and defying him, vanishing so he could fall asleep at last, and the moment oblivion had engulfed him reappearing and waking him by a sharp spasm of jealousy.

He left his bed at the first hour of dawn and walked out into the forest carrying a cane, a heavy one forgotten in his new house by the last inhabitant. The rising sun fell through the nearly naked treetops onto the earth carpeted in places by bright green grass, farther on by patches of dead leaves, then with thickets reddened by the winter; yellow butterflies fluttered along the path like tiny dancing flames. A great hill, almost a mountain, covered with pines and bluish rocks, appeared to his right. Mariolle climbed it slowly, and when he had reached the summit, sat on a boulder, already panting. His legs were giving way under him, his heart was pounding; his whole body seemed to ache with an inconceivable exhaustion. This collapse, he could tell, was not the result of fatigue: it came from Her and from that love pressing on him like an intolerable weight, and he murmured, "What misery! Why does she have such a grip on me? I who never asked more of life than to enjoy it without suffering?"

His overexcited attention, sharpened by fear of this pain which might prove so difficult to overcome, turned inward. He dug deep, striving to learn, to understand better, to bring to light the reason for this inexplicable crisis.

He lectured himself. "I've never been carried away. I'm not a fanatic, I'm hardly a passionate man; I have more judgment than instinct, more curiosity than appetite, more imagination than perseverance. All I am, really, is a sensitive, intelligent, fastidious voluptuary. I've enjoyed the good things of life without ever being desperately attached to them—have the senses of a wine taster who savors without drinking too deeply, a man who knows too much to lose his head. I reason everything out, and usually analyze my tastes too well to succumb to them blindly. And that's my chief defect, the real cause of my weakness. But this woman has taken possession of me in spite of myself, in spite of my fear and my knowledge of her; and she possesses me as if she had plucked out, one after the other, my every last aspiration. Maybe that's what it is. Here I was turning my ambitions toward abstract things, toward music, which is a kind of ideal caress, toward nature, which allures me and touches me, toward thinking, which is really the mind's gluttony, and toward everything on earth which is pleasant and lovely. And then I encounter a creature who combines all my rather hesitant and volatile desires, and by focusing them on herself has converted them into love. Elegant and lovely, she delights my eyes; subtle, intelligent, and clever, she delights my soul; and she delights my heart by the mysterious pleasure of her contact and her presence, by some secret and irresistible emanation of her person which has conquered me like a gorgeous and stupefying flower. She has taken the place of everything; there is nothing I aspire to now, I need nothing, I want nothing, I care for nothing. Before she came, how I should have quivered with enjoyment at the spectacle of this forest reborn with the spring! Today I scarcely see it, I fail to feel it, I'm not in it; I'm always with her, this woman I no longer want to love. Up then, forward, onward! I must kill such ideas by exhausting them, otherwise I'll never be cured."

He stood up, climbed down the rocky hill, and continued walking, taking great strides. But his obsession weighed on him, as if he were carrying a great burden. He walked faster and faster, occasionally encountering, at the sight of the sun plunging through the new leaves or at a whiff of resin from a grove of pines, a swift sensation of relief, like the presentiment of some remote consolation. Suddenly he stopped. "I'm no longer walking," he told himself, "I'm fleeing." It was true, he was fleeing, fleeing ahead, fleeing anywhere; he was fleeing, pursued by the anguish of his broken love. Then he began walking more calmly. The forest changed its appearance, becoming deeper and shadier; he was entering its warm heart, penetrating a brilliant grove of beeches. No vestige of winter remained; so fresh and young was the spring it seemed to have been born the night before.

Mariolle made his way through the thickets under huge trees which rose higher and higher, and walked straight ahead for an hour, two hours, through undergrowth, through countless multitudes of shiny little leaves, each glistening with new life. The sky was hidden by the huge vault of the treetops, supported by tall columns, straight or leaning, sometimes whitish, sometimes dark, where black moss grew on the bark. Soaring trunks rose in close ranks all around him, surrounded by a tangled new growth of underbrush blanketing them with a dense cloud occasionally pierced by cataracts of sunlight, a rain of fire slithered and flowed throughout this foliage which no longer seemed a forest at all but rather a brilliant green mist flecked with golden rays.

Mariolle stopped walking, overcome by amazement. Where was he? In a forest or in the depths of an ocean of leaves and light, a sea gilded with green luminescence? He felt better now, calmer as he left his misery behind; hidden from it, he lay down on the russet carpet of dead leaves the trees relinquished only when they had covered themselves with new foliage. Relishing the contact of the earth and of the pure sweetness of the air, he was soon overcome by a desire, vague at first, then more specific, not to be alone in this enchanted spot, and he said to himself, "Ah, if only she were here with me!"

Suddenly the vision of Mont-Saint-Michel flashed before his eyes, and remembering how different she had been there from what she was in Paris, in that dawning affection roused by the sea breeze sweeping across the pale sands, it seemed to him that on that day alone had she loved him a little, for a few hours...Certainly, on the road, following the receding tides, in the cloister where she murmured his first name, "André," she seemed to be saying "I'm yours," and on the Madman's Walk where he had virtually carried her in his arms, she had felt some sort of rapture, something that had never recurred since her coquettish foot had touched the pavements of Paris. But here, with him, in this bath of green, this other tide of new life, wouldn't those sweet and fleeting emotions have regained their hold on her heart, the same joys that had awakened on the coast of Normandy?

He lay stretched out on his back, still vanquished by his memories, or were they only dreams? His gaze wandered through the sun-drenched treetops, and in a little while he managed to close his eyes, benumbed beneath the great calm of the trees. Finally he slept, and when he wakened he realized it must be after two in the afternoon. He got up feeling a little less sad, a little less sick, and walked on. At last he emerged from the heart of the woods and entered a broad crossroads where six avenues, intersecting like the points of a crown, melted into transparent distances in the emerald air. A signpost indicated the name of the place: The King's Bouquet. Here indeed was the capital, the capital of the Kingdom of the Beeches.

An empty carriage passed. Mariolle hailed it and rode as far as Marlotte, planning to walk from there to Montigny, after eating lunch at the inn, for he was suddenly hungry. He remembered having passed this newly opened establishment the day before: Hôtel Corot, Café Artiste, with medieval decorations on the model of the Chat Noir in Paris. He walked through an open door into a vast hall where old-fashioned tables and uncomfortable stools seemed to be waiting for revelers from a bygone age. At the far end of the room, a young woman standing on the top rung of a short ladder was hanging old plates on nails too high for her to reach. Sometimes with both feet on tiptoe and sometimes just one, she held one hand against a nail in the wall, the other sliding a plate to hang from it, her body making graceful movements while performing this task, for her waist was slender and the undulating lines from her wrist down to her ankle kept changing with each of her efforts. Her back was to him, and she failed to hear Mariolle walk in and stand watching her. He remembered Prédolé's observations and thought to himself, "How pretty that child is in just that pose!" He coughed, and she was so startled that she nearly fell, but once she recovered her balance, she jumped to the floor from the top of the ladder with the lightness of an acrobat and came smiling toward the client. "Monsieur would like...?"

"Lunch, mademoiselle."

"It would have to be dinner, it's three thirty."

"Dinner then, if you like. I got lost in the forest."

She listed the available dishes; he made his choice and sat down at a table. She went to the kitchen, then returned to set his place. He watched her, admiring her neatness and grace. Dressed for work, her sleeves rolled up, her neck bare, she had a pleasant, alert expression, and her blouse closely followed the curves of her delicate waist, of which she was doubtless quite proud. Flushed by the country air, her face seemed a little too plump, but it had the freshness of an opening flower, and her fine brown eyes seemed to glow like everything else in her countenance, her open mouth full of splendid teeth and her chestnut hair, its very abundance suggesting the vitality of this vigorous young body.

She brought radishes and butter, and he began to eat, no longer watching her. To drown his thoughts he ordered a bottle of champagne and drank it all, as well as two glasses of kümmel after his coffee; and since he had drunk his champagne on an empty stomach, he felt himself invaded and comforted by an intense giddiness which he took for forgetfulness. His ideas, his distress, his anguish seemed diluted, then drowned in the bright wine which had so rapidly turned his tormented heart into a nearly inert one. He walked slowly back to his new house in Montigny where he went to bed as soon as it grew dark and fell asleep immediately. But he awoke in pitch darkness, uneasy, tormented as if a nightmare routed some hours ago had stealthily returned to interrupt his sleep. She was there, Madame de Burne, still prowling around, still accompanied by Count de Bernhaus. "So I'm jealous now," he said to himself. "Why should I be?"

Why was he jealous? He soon understood why. Despite his fears and his anxieties, as long as he was her lover he believed her to be faithful to him, faithful without enthusiasm, without tenderness, but with a loyal resolve. But now that he had broken everything off, he had liberated her: it was over. Would she remain without a lover now? Yes, very probably, for a while. And then . . . ? That same fidelity which it had never occurred to him to doubt—wasn't it really caused by the vague presentiment that if she wearied of him, inevitably it would come about, one day or another, after an intermission of whatever length, that she would replace him, not because of some fascination but rather from the fatigue of solitude, as she would have rejected him eventually because she was tired of his attachment. Are there not lovers who are retained for better or worse, with resignation, out of fear of *the next*? Besides, merely exchanging one pair of arms for another would not have seemed correct behavior to a woman like Madame de Burne, too intelligent to be troubled by such prejudicial judgments as disgrace and dishonor, but endowed with a delicate moral modesty which would protect her from actual defilement. A worldly philosopher rather than a bourgeois prude, she would hardly shrink from a secret attachment, but her indifferent flesh would have shuddered with disgust at the thought of a succession of lovers.

He had set her free . . . and now? Now, certainly, she would take another! And it would be Count de Bernhaus. Mariolle was certain of it, and suffered indescribably from the certitude.

Why had he broken off with her? He had left her knowing she was faithful, friendly, charming! Why then? Because he was a sensual brute who knew nothing of love without its physical applications? Was that it? Yes . . . But there was something more!

There was, above and beyond that deprivation, the dread of suffering. He had fled the pain of not being loved as *he* loved, the cruel divergence which had arisen between them, the unequal tenderness of their kisses, the incurable pain from which his heart, rudely smitten, would never be free. He had been afraid of suffering too much, of enduring for years the anguish of several weeks which had seemed like months to him. Weak, as always, he had shrunk from such suffering, just as all his life he had shrunk from truly great efforts.

That was it: he was incapable of carrying anything to its conclusion, of flinging himself into passion as he ought to have flung himself into science, into art, for perhaps it is impossible to have greatly loved without having greatly suffered. Till dawn he was a victim of such ideas which gnawed his conscience like so many dogs; then he got up and walked down to the river. A fisherman was casting his net near the weir. The water glistened in the early light, and when the man drew up his big round net to spread it out on the stern of his boat, the slender minnows squirmed in the meshes like quicksilver. Mariolle calmed down as the morning air grew warmer and a mist rose above the little waterfall where tiny rainbows danced; the current flowing at his feet seemed to carry away some of his distress in its swift incessant flight. He comforted himself: "I did the right thing; I'd have suffered too much!"

Returning to the house, he got the hammock he had noticed in the vestibule and hung it between two lindens, and climbing in, tried to empty his mind as he watched the stream race past. He ate his breakfast in a gentle torpor, a physical well-being that also reached his soul, and he made the slight meal last as long as possible to slow down the day's passing. But waiting for the mail made him anxious; he had wired to Paris and written to Fontainebleau for his letters to be sent on. Nothing had arrived, and the sensation of abandonment began to oppress him. Why? There was nothing pleasant, consoling, reassuring to be hoped for in the little black box on the postman's hip, nothing but useless invitations and banal communications. So why long for those unknown pages if his heart's salvation were inside them? Was he not concealing from himself the selfish hope that she might write to him? He asked one of the old women, "What time does the mail come?"

"At noon, monsieur."

The moment was upon him, and he listened for the noises outside with mounting anxiety. A knock on the front door relieved his tension, but the postman brought nothing but newspapers and three unimportant letters. Mariolle read and reread the papers, grew bored, and left the house. What was he to do? He returned to the hammock and stretched out once again, but after half an hour an imperious need to do something seized him. The forest? Yes, the forest was delicious, but the solitude there seemed deeper than in his house or the village, where at least some sounds of life could occasionally be heard. And that silent solitude of the trees and the leaves filled him with melancholy regret, would drown him in his wretchedness. He repeated mentally his long walk of the day before, and at the memory of the alert little waitress he reassured himself, "That's what I'll do, I'll go there and have dinner!" The very thought of it consoled him; it was something to do, a means of moving through time, and he set out on his way.

The long village street led straight into the valley between its two rows of low houses with their white-tiled roofs, the ones on the left close to the road, those on the other side behind little courtyards where lilacs bloomed, or chickens pecked in the dung heap, or flights of wooden stairs led up to doorways in the wall. Peasants were working slowly around their houses at various domestic tasks; a bent old woman with grayish-yellow hair despite her age—country people almost never have really white hair—passed close by him in a ragged old blouse, her knobby, skinny legs clearly outlined under a scanty woolen skirt. She stared straight ahead with eyes that had never seen anything but the eight or ten objects necessary to her wretched existence. A younger woman was hanging laundry out to dry in front of her door. The movement of her arms raised her skirt, revealing thick ankles in blue stockings and the bony legs above them, while her waist and chest, wide and flat as a man's, indicated a shapeless, repulsive body. Mariolle thought, "Women! These are women!" The figure of Madame de Burne flashed before his eyes, exquisite in elegance and beauty, a gem of human flesh embellished for the satisfaction of men's eyes, and he shuddered with the anguish of an irreparable loss. He walked on quickly to change his thoughts and distract his heart. When he reached the Hôtel Corot, the little waitress recognized him immediately and greeted him almost familiarly: "Good day, monsieur."

"Good day, mademoiselle."

"Would you like something to drink?"

"Yes, for a start; then I'll have dinner." They discussed what he would drink first, and what he would eat afterward. He consulted her in order to make her speak, for she expressed herself nicely, with the crisp accent of Paris and an ease of elocution that was as graceful as her movements. He thought, "How pretty she is, she has the makings of a real cocotte," and he asked her, "You're a Parisian, aren't you?"

"Yes, monsieur."

"Have you been here long?"

"Two weeks, monsieur."

"Do you like it?"

"Not so far, but it's too soon to decide; besides, I had enough of the city, and the country air is doing me good. That's really what made me come. Shall I bring you a glass of vermouth, monsieur?"

"Yes, mademoiselle, and please tell the chef or the cook to do his or her best with my dinner."

"Have no fear, monsieur." And she went out of the room, leaving him alone. He walked into the hotel garden and sat at a table under a sort of arbor, where his vermouth was served. He stayed there till the end of the day, listening to a thrush whistling in its cage and occasionally watching his waitress, who did her best to please this gentleman who obviously found her to his taste. As had happened the day before, Mariolle left the establishment with a bottle of champagne warming his heart; but the shadows of the road and the coolness of the evening quickly dispelled his slight intoxication, and once again an invincible melancholy filled his soul. He thought, "What'll I do? Stay here? How long am I doomed to drag out this miserable existence?" And he went to bed very late.

The next day, he was rocking again in his hammock, when the constant presence of the man casting his net gave him the idea of going fishing for himself. A grocer sold him the lines and gave him some tips on the gentle sport, even offering to supervise his first attempts. The proposition was accepted, and between nine in the morning and noon Mariolle, with enormous effort and great concentration, managed to land three tiny fish.

After his meal, he returned to Marlotte. Why? To pass the time. The little waitress, catching sight of him, burst out laughing. He smiled back, amused by this salutation, and attempted to make her talk to him. And she talked, more familiarly than the day before. Her name was Élisabeth Ledru. Her mother, a dressmaker, had died a year ago; then her father, a bookkeeper, always drunk and usually out of work, disappeared; it had become clear to him that the girl, alone all day sewing in her attic, could never support the two of them by her efforts. Exhausted in due time by her solitary labors, she had signed on as a waitress in a cheap restaurant, remained there a year, and when she tired of the city, she accepted the offer of the new manager of the Hôtel Corot, whom she was serving, to go to Marlotte and wait on tables for the summer with two other girls who would be coming later. Obviously the manager knew how to attract a clientele.

The story pleased Mariolle, who by questioning the girl carefully and treating her like a lady learned a good deal about her grim attic life ruined by a drunkard's folly. This child, a lost waif but gay nonetheless because of her youth, sensing this stranger's genuine interest and his lively attention, spoke quite trustingly and with a sincerity she could no more conceal than she could the grace of her limbs.

When she finished he asked her, "And . . . you'll go on being a waitress all your life?"

"I don't know, monsieur. How can I tell what will happen tomorrow or the next day?"

"Still, it's always best to plan for the future."

She looked thoughtful for a moment, then her face cleared and she said, "I'll take whatever comes my way, you know how it is." They parted good friends.

He returned a couple of days later, then once again, then often, vaguely drawn by the naïve confidences of this abandoned girl whose simple chatter comforted his own grim thoughts. Yet when he walked back to Montigny in the evening, he would find himself thinking of Madame de Burne and visited by dreadful fits of despair. With each dawn, his heart revived a little, but by nightfall the lacerating regrets and fierce jealousy returned. He had no news. He had written to no one, and no one had written to him. He knew nothing. Then, alone on the dark forest road, he imagined the progress of the imminent liaison he had foreseen between his former mistress and Count de Bernhaus. This obsession ate deeper into him every day. A man like that, he thought, will give her what she wants: a distinguished affair with an assiduous, undemanding lover, satisfied and flattered to be the choice of this delicious and witty coquette. He compared the count to himself. Bernhaus, certainly, would reveal nothing like his exasperation, those tiresome bouts of impatience, that painful need for mutual tenderness which had destroyed their love affair, if that was what it had been. He would be content with little enough, this man of the world, so flexible, so tactful, so discreet, unlikely to be a victim of his own passions.

Then one day, as André Mariolle arrived at Marlotte, he glimpsed beneath one of the Hôtel Corot's arbors two young bearded fellows wearing berets and smoking pipes. The *patron*, a stout man with a rosy countenance, immediately came to greet him, for he had developed a sympathetic interest in this loyal guest, and then quite casually remarked, "We have two new clients, did you notice? They arrived yesterday."

"The two men over there?"

"Yes, they're quite well-known painters. The shorter one got his second medal last year." And having told all he knew of these budding artists, he asked, "What will you have today, Monsieur Mariolle?"

"Send over a vermouth when you have a chance, as usual."

The *patron* left, and in a minute or two Élisabeth came outside carrying a tray with a glass, a decanter, and a bottle. And as soon as she appeared, one of the painters shouted, "Hey, little girl, are you still pissed at us?"

She made no answer, and when she stood beside Mariolle he noticed that her eyes were red. "Have you been crying?" he asked.

She answered simply, "Yes, a little."

"What happened?"

"Those two gentlemen over there were... mean to me."

"What did they do?"

"They treated me like... something I'm not."

"Did you complain to the *patron*?"

She gave a despairing shrug. "Oh! Monsieur... the *patron*... the *patron*... I know him... now, the *patron*..."

Mariolle, moved and a little annoyed, said, "Tell me exactly what happened." She described the immediate and brutal efforts of the two daubers who had arrived the day before. Then she began crying all over again, wondering what she was going to do, a girl without money or friends in this strange place.

Mariolle suddenly made her an offer. "How would you like to work for me? You would be well treated at my place, and then when I go back to Paris, you'll be free to do what you like."

She stared at him for a moment, and then said abruptly, "I'd like that, monsieur."

"How much do you make here?"

"Sixty francs a month." And then she added, suddenly anxious: "And then there's my share of the tips. It comes to about seventy."

"I'll pay you a hundred."

Astonished, she repeated, "A hundred francs a month?"

"Yes. Will that suit you?"

"Of course it will."

"Your job will be to work in my kitchen, to take care of my clothes and do the laundry, and to keep my bedroom clean."

"That will be fine, monsieur."

"When can you start?"

"Tomorrow, if you like. After what happened here, I'll go see the mayor—he'll make the *patron* let me go."

Mariolle took two louis d'or out of his pocket and handed them to her, saying, "Here's a little something for good luck."

Her face lit up, and she said in a firm tone of voice, "I'll be at your place tomorrow before noon, monsieur."

2

ÉLISABETH arrived at Montigny the next morning, followed by a peasant carrying her trunk in a wheelbarrow. Mariolle had discharged one of his old women with a generous tip, and the newcomer took possession of a little bedroom on the second floor, next to the cook's. When she presented herself to her employer, she struck him as somewhat different from what she had been at Marlotte, less expansive, humbler now that she was the servant of the gentleman who had befriended her under the arbor of the Hôtel Corot. He indicated in a few words what her duties would be. She listened carefully, put away her things, and got to work.

A week went by with no appreciable change in Mariolle's spirit. All he noticed was that he left his house less frequently, for he no longer had the excuse of excursions to Marlotte, and the place seemed perhaps less gloomy than during the first days of his occupancy. The intensity of his grief had somewhat lessened, as everything does; but instead of that turbulence, an insurmountable melancholy possessed him, one of those profound depressions like the slow and chronic diseases which so frequently prove to be fatal. All his former activity, all the curiosity of his mind, all his interest in the things by which he had hitherto been challenged and amused were dead within him, replaced by a universal disgust and an insuperable indifference which left him not even the strength to get up and take a walk. He rarely left the house now, merely shifting from his living room to his hammock, and from his hammock to his living room. His major distractions consisted of watching the Loing flow past and the fisherman cast his net.

After her first days of shyness and reserve, Élisabeth grew a little bolder, and noticing her master's constant depression, she asked him now and then, when the other servant was not there, "Is monsieur feeling out of sorts?"

He would answer with resignation, "Yes, a little, maybe."

"Perhaps monsieur should go for a walk."

"That wouldn't do me much good."

She lavished little secret attentions upon him. Each morning, when he came into the salon, he would find it full of flowers and fragrant as a hothouse. Élisabeth must have commissioned the village boys to bring her primroses and violets from the forest and laid the village gardens under contribution as well. For all his torpor and his melancholy, Mariolle couldn't help noticing this ingenious form of gratitude and the concern for him she revealed in many thoughtful attentions.

It also struck him that she was growing prettier, more attentive to her appearance—her face seemed paler now, actually more refined. He even observed, one day, as she was serving his tea, that her hands were no longer those of a servant but a lady's hands, with irreproachably clean manicured nails. On another occasion he realized that her shoes were almost elegant. Then, one afternoon, when she had gone upstairs to her room, she came back down in a charming little gray dress, simple and in perfect taste. "Good Lord, Élisabeth," he exclaimed, "what a flirt you've become!"

She blushed to the roots of her hair and stammered, "Me? Oh no, monsieur. I'm dressing a little better now because I have a little more money."

"Where did you buy a dress like that?"

"I made it myself, monsieur."

"You made it? When did you do that? I see you working all day long around the house."

"In the evening, monsieur."

"And the material—where did you get that? And who cut the pattern for you?"

She explained that the dry-goods shopkeeper in Montigny had brought her some samples from Fontainebleau. She had made her choice and paid for the merchandise with the two louis d'or Mariolle had given her. As for cutting the cloth and choosing the style of the dress, there was no difficulty about that after working with her mother as a dressmaker all those years.

He couldn't help saying, "It's very becoming, Élisabeth. You look very nice indeed."

She blushed again, perhaps a little more deeply than before. When she left the room, he wondered, "Could she be falling in love with me?" He thought it over, hesitated, doubted, and ended by convincing himself it was possible after all. He had been kind, sympathetic, helpful, almost a friend. What was surprising about this child having taken a shine to her master after what he had done for her? Moreover the notion didn't strike him as unpleasant at all, the little creature was really quite appealing, there was nothing of a servant about her any more. His male vanity, so offended, so wounded, so crushed by another woman, felt soothed, flattered, almost comforted. It was a compensation, a very slight, almost imperceptible one, but a compensation nevertheless, for when love is shown for someone, whatever the source, it proves that such a person can inspire love. His unconscious egoism was satisfied as well. It would occupy his mind, and perhaps do him some good to watch this little heart awaken and begin to beat for him. It never once occurred to him to send the girl away, to preserve her from the very danger from which he was suffering so cruelly himself—to have more pity on her than had been shown to him. Compassion has no part to play in sentimental victories.

So he observed her, and soon realized he had not been mistaken. Every day tiny details confirmed his theory. When she brushed against him while serving breakfast one morning, he detected perfume in her clothes—a cheap perfume, doubtless provided by the shopkeeper or the pharmacist. And he took the occasion to give her a bottle of eau de toilette of a kind he himself had used for years and always kept in plentiful supply when away from home. He also gave her several cakes of fine soap, some dentifrice, and a box of rice powder. He was subtly, or perhaps not so subtly, assisting in her transformation, daily more apparent, daily more complete, following it with a watchful and flattered scrutiny. While remaining a faithful and discreet servant, she was becoming an aroused, enamored woman whose every coquettish instinct was naïvely developing.

He himself was gradually growing attached to her. He was amused, touched, and grateful. He toyed with this nascent tenderness as one toys, on sad occasions, with any available diversion. He felt no other attraction to her than that vague desire which impels a man toward any pretty woman, a good-looking waitress or a peasant girl with the lineaments of a goddess. What drew him to her most of all was a sort of nonspecific *odore di femmina*. That was his need now, a confused and irresistible need aroused in him by that other woman whom he loved and who had awakened in him an invincible and mysterious longing for the presence, the contact, the subtle aroma of women, ideal or sensual, which for men in whom the immemorial allure of the feminine still survives is the characteristic attribute of any seductive creature, whatever her race or nation, whatever her type or class.

This tender, incessant, caressing secret attention—more intuited than recognized—protected his wound like a layer of protective cotton wool, so that it became a little less sensitive to the recurring attacks of his anguish. They subsisted nonetheless, fluttering like flies around an open sore. It was enough for one of them to land for him to begin suffering all over again. Since he had not divulged his address to anyone, his friends respected his seclusion, and he was particularly tormented by the lack of news and information. From time to time he would read in a newspaper the names Lamarthe or Massival in the guest list of some grand dinner. One day he saw Madame de Burne's name, cited as among the most elegant and best-dressed women at a ball given by the Austrian embassy. A shudder ran through his whole body.

The name of Count de Bernhaus appeared a few lines farther down the column, and all that day Mariolle's heart was riven by jealousy. This presumed liaison was now established beyond a doubt in his mind! It was one of those imaginary convictions, more troubling than any actual fact, impossible to get rid of or get over.

Unable to bear any longer this complete ignorance and this uncertainty in his suspicions, he decided to write to Lamarthe, who knowing him well enough to guess his misery might address his suppositions, even without being directly questioned. One evening, then, he wrote him a letter, a long, cleverly phrased, vaguely melancholy screed, full of veiled interrogations and lyrical rhapsodies on the beauty of springtime in the country. In his mail four days later, he recognized at first glance the novelist's firm, perpendicular handwriting; Lamarthe had sent him a thousand distressing details, to which his anxieties were particularly vulnerable. He mentioned a great many people, but without giving more emphasis to Madame de Burne and Bernhaus than to anyone else in particular, he seemed to focus on the two of them by one of those tricks of style which were so typical of him and which drew his reader's attention just where he wanted it to be without revealing that he was doing anything of the kind. Consequently his letter made it clear that all of Mariolle's suspicions were at the very least well-founded. His apprehensions would be realized tomorrow, had they not already been so the day before yesterday. His former mistress's life was the same as it had always been—brilliant, exciting, worldly. As for Mariolle himself, there had been quite a lot of talk about him after his disappearance, the way people always talk about such things—with a sort of indifferent curiosity. People believed he was somewhere far away, his mysterious departure caused by his disillusionment with Paris.

After receiving this letter, Mariolle remained stretched out in his hammock until evening. He couldn't eat; he couldn't sleep; and that night he had a fever. The next day he felt so exhausted, so discouraged, so disgusted by the monotonous days between this silent forest quite black with foliage by now and the garrulous little river flowing under his windows that he couldn't get out of bed.

When Élisabeth came to his room at the sound of his bell and found him still in bed, she stood in the open doorway, suddenly pale, and asked, "Monsieur is ill?"

"Yes, a little."

"Should I send for the doctor?"

"No. I have these attacks now and then."

"What does monsieur need?"

He ordered his daily bath, eggs for breakfast, and tea throughout the day. But toward one o'clock he was overcome by such a violent sensation of tedium that he realized he must get up. Élisabeth, ceaselessly summoned by the whims of this sham invalid and promptly answering his calls with an anxious, saddened expression, eager to be useful and afford relief, to care for him and cure his malady, seeing him so agitated and nervous, offered— blushing at her own audacity—to read to him, anything he liked.

"Can you read well?" he asked.

"Yes, monsieur. In the city schools I was awarded all the prizes for reading, and I used to read novels to Mama—I read so many I can't remember anything but their names now."

His curiosity aroused, he sent her to the studio to find, among the books that he had requested to be sent to him, the one he preferred to all others, *Manon Lescaut*. Then she helped him sit up in bed, arranged two pillows behind his back, took a chair, and began. It was true that she read well, very well in fact, possessing a real gift for correct pronunciation and intelligent expression. The story interested her from the start, and she read on with so much feeling that he occasionally interrupted her performance to ask questions and make her talk a little.

Through the open window, the warm breeze bearing the scent of the spring forest also carried the trills and chirps of the nightingales singing to their mates in this season of returning loves. André watched the girl as she read, her shining eyes following the lines of the story from page to page. To the questions he asked, she replied with an apparently innate understanding of passion and tenderness, though perhaps slightly confused by her inexperience. And he thought, "With a little education this child would become quite intelligent and even subtle." The feminine charm he had discerned in her was doing him some good this calm, warm afternoon, and it mingled strangely in his mind with the mysterious and potent allure of that Manon, whose womanly allure strikes the heart more strangely than any other evoked by human art. Lulled by the voice, seduced by the familiar and ever-fresh tale, he dreamed of a capricious and captivating mistress like des Grieux's, unfaithful and constant, human and so tempting in even her worst faults, created to elicit from a man whatever he can produce of tenderness and rage, of attachment and passionate hatred, of jealousy and desire. Ah! If only the woman he had just fled had had in her veins the loving and sensual perfidy of that exasperating courtesan, perhaps he would never have left her! Manon cheated, but she loved; she lied, but she gave herself!

After that slothful day, Mariolle relaxed, by evening, into a kind of dreamy state in which all the women he had ever known melted together. Having done nothing since the day before, nor made even the slightest movement, he slept lightly, troubled by unaccustomed noises somewhere in the house.

Once or twice already, during the nights, he had thought he made out barely perceptible movements downstairs, not right below him but in the little rooms off the kitchen: the laundry and the bathroom. He had paid no particular attention. But tonight, tired of lying down, incapable of falling back to sleep after many attempts, he listened carefully and distinguished inexplicable rustling sounds and a sort of splashing. Then he made up his mind to solve the mystery, lit his candle, looked at the time: not even ten o'clock. He got dressed, put a revolver in his pocket, and tiptoed downstairs with infinite precautions. Entering the kitchen, he was astonished to see that the stove was lit. There were no further noises, but he thought he detected some sort of movement in the bathroom, a tiny whitewashed room containing only a bathtub.

He approached, turned the knob without making a sound, and suddenly pushing open the door, discovered lying in the water, her arms floating and the tips of her breasts breaking the surface, the loveliest woman's body he had ever seen in his life. She uttered a little scream of terror, being quite unable to escape. Already he was kneeling beside the tub, devouring her with eager eyes, his lips stretched toward her. She understood, and suddenly raising her dripping arms, Élisabeth closed them around her employer's head.

3

WHEN SHE appeared before him the next morning, carrying the tea tray, and their eyes met, she began trembling so violently that the cup and saucer and the sugar bowl started rattling together. Mariolle went toward her, took the tray from her hands, set it on the table, and said to her, as she lowered her eyes, "Look at me, child." She looked at him, her lashes wet with tears. "I don't want you to cry."

As he drew her against him, he felt her entire body trembling, and she murmured, "Oh my God!" He realized that it was not pain, nor regret, nor remorse that made her stammer these three words, but happiness, true happiness. And in him there was a strange, selfish contentment, physical rather than moral, as he felt nestling against his chest this little person who finally loved him.

He thanked her for it as a wounded man, aided by a passing woman, would offer thanks; he thanked her with his whole lacerated heart, betrayed in so many futile impulses, starved for tenderness by another's indifference; and from the depths of that injured heart he pitied her a little. Looking at her now, pale and tearful, her eyes shining with love, he suddenly realized: "But she's beautiful! How quickly a woman is transformed, becomes what she must be, according to the desires of her soul or the needs of her life!"

"Sit down," he said to her. She sat down and he took her hands, the poor hands of a working girl that had become white and delicate for him, and very gently, with careful phrases, he spoke to her of the way they would treat each other now. She was no longer his servant, but would keep something of the appearance of that condition, in order to avoid a scandal in the village. She would live with him as his housekeeper, and would frequently read to him, which would serve as an excuse in their new situation. In a short while, when her function as his reader was quite well established, she would eat at his table.

When he had finished speaking, she answered simply, "No, monsieur: I am your servant, and I shall be your servant. I don't want people gossiping, and no one needs to know what has happened." She would not yield on the point, though he insisted a good deal, and when he had drunk his tea, she took the tray away, followed by his tender glance. Once she had left, he reflected: "She's a woman. All women are alike when they please us. I've made my servant my mistress. She's pretty, she may become charming. In any case, she's fresher and younger than society women, than cocottes. What does it matter, after all! How many famous actresses are concierges' daughters? And they're received like ladies, worshipped like heroines in novels, and princes treat them like sovereigns. Is that because of their often dubious talent, or their often questionable beauty? No. But a woman's situation is always determined by the illusion she produces."

That day he took a long walk, and though deep in his heart he still felt the same pain, and his legs were as heavy as if grief had strained all the springs of his energy, something hummed within him like the faint song of a bird. He was less alone, less lost, less abandoned. The forest seemed less empty, less silent, less black. He returned home longing to see Élisabeth coming toward him, smiling at his approach, her eyes filled with tenderness.

For almost a month it was a real idyll on the bank of the little river. Mariolle was loved as very few men perhaps have been loved, creaturely and wildly, like a child by its mother, like a hunter by his dog. He was everything for her, heaven and earth, pleasure and happiness. He fulfilled all her ardent and naïve expectations, giving her in a kiss all she could know of ecstasy. She had only André in her gaze, in her soul, in her heart, and in her flesh, intoxicated like an adolescent drinking for the first time. He fell asleep in her arms, he awoke to her caresses, and she explored with him unimaginable embraces. Surprised and seduced, he relished this absolute offering, and he had the impression that this was love tasted at its very source, drunk from nature's lips.

Yet he remained melancholy all the while, melancholy and disenchanted. The condition was constant and profound. His young mistress delighted him, but he missed the other one. And when he walked in the meadows, along the banks of the Loing, wondering "Why this never-ending tribulation?," he found in himself, whenever the memory of Paris touched him, a restiveness so intolerable that he would return home in order not to be alone a moment longer.

Then he would rock himself in the hammock, and Élisabeth, sitting on a stool, would read to him. Listening to her, looking at her, he remembered those conversations in his former mistress's salon, when he would spend his evenings alone beside her. Then an abominable need to cry would moisten his eyelids; his heart was racked by a regret so intense that he would feel the craving to leave at that moment become intolerable. He would have to return to Paris or go away forever.

Seeing him depressed and melancholy, Élisabeth would ask, "Are you sick again? I can see you have tears in your eyes."

And he would answer, "Kiss me, child. It's something you wouldn't understand."

And she would kiss him, anxious, aware of some drama she could not fathom. But he, forgetting his misery a little in her caresses, would think, "Ah, a woman who would be the two of them, who would have this one's love and that one's charm! Why do we never find the reality of our dreams and always meet with approximations?" He mused on, lulled by that monotonous sound of her voice to which he wasn't listening, recalling all that had captivated him, conquered him, in his forsaken mistress, and in the obsessive memory of her imaginary presence, he asked himself, "Am I a damned soul who will never be free of her?"

He went back to taking long walks, prowling the glades with a dim hope of losing her somewhere, deep in a ravine, behind a boulder, tangled in some thicket—like a man who to rid himself of a faithful animal he cannot bear to kill, tries to lose it by taking a long excursion in the remote fastnesses of the forest.

One day, at the end of one of these walks, he found himself back among the beeches. It was now a dark, almost pitch-black forest of impenetrable foliage. He walked beneath the huge vault, moist and cavernous, regretting the faint green transparency of the scarcely opened new leaves, and suddenly stopped, astonished, on the narrow path, in front of two interlaced trees. No image of his love more violent and more moving could have struck his eyes and his soul: a vigorous beech embracing a sapling oak.

Like a desperate lover with a powerful and tormented body, the beech twisted two huge wormlike branches around the young oak's trunk. The oak, held in this embrace, reached toward the sky, well above the aggressor's body, slender and supple and seemingly disdainful. Yet despite this flight into space, the haughty evasion of an outraged victim, it bore in its side two deep scars which the irresistible beech branches had gashed into its bark. Sealed together forever by these closed wounds, the trees grew into each other, mixing their sap, and in the veins of the violated flowed and rose to its lofty summit the lifeblood of the vanquisher.

Mariolle sat down and contemplated them for a long while. They became symbolic, in his sick soul: dreadful and superb, these two motionless combatants who told to passing strangers the eternal story of his love. Then he walked on, sadder than ever, and suddenly, as he did so, eyes on the ground and advancing slowly, he noticed, half hidden in the grass, stained by mud and rain, an old telegram, lost or discarded by someone who had been walking here. He stopped. What message, something painful or dear to some heart, was left on this scrap of blue paper lying at his feet?

He couldn't help picking it up, and with curious and reluctant fingers unfolded it. It was still almost legible: "Come... me... four o'clock." The names had been washed away by the moisture of the path. Memories swarmed through his mind, cruel and delicious, phrases of all the telegrams he had ever received from her, sometimes to arrange a meeting, sometimes to tell him she wasn't coming. Nothing had ever aroused stronger feelings in him, had made his poor heart pound faster than the sight of those enthralling or desolating messages. He remained almost prostrate with discouragement at the realization that he would never open one of these ever again. Again he wondered what had happened to her, within her, since he had left her. Had she suffered, regretted the friend driven away by her indifference, or had she taken his abandonment in stride, no more than a trivial wound to her vanity? And his craving to know became so violent, so gripping, that a bold and bizarre thought flashed through his mind. He took the road to Fontainebleau. When he reached the town, he went to the telegraph office, his soul shaken by vacillation and anxiety. But he seemed driven by an irresistible force now. He picked up a form on the table and on it, below the name and address of Madame Michèle de Burne, he wrote:

I HAVE A TERRIBLE NEED TO KNOW WHAT YOU THINK OF ME. I CAN FORGET NOTHING. ANDRÉ MARIOLLE. MONTIGNY.

Then he left the office, hailed a fiacre, and returned to Montigny, troubled and tormented by what he had done, already regretting it. He calculated that if she deigned to reply, he would receive her letter two days later; but even so he did not leave his villa the next day, hoping and dreading to receive a message from her.

Around three in the afternoon, he was rocking in his hammock under the lindens on the terrace, when Élisabeth came to tell him that there was a lady who wanted to speak to him.

His excitement was so great that he had a sudden choking fit, and walked toward the house with a pounding heart and tingling legs. Yet he did not suppose it could be Madame de Burne.

When he opened the living-room door, she was sitting on a couch, but she stood up at once, smiling a rather tense smile, with a certain constraint in her expression and her posture. She held out her hand and said, "I came for some real news, the telegram wasn't quite enough." He had turned so pale at seeing her that her eyes shone with joy; and he remained so overcome with emotion that he couldn't speak and merely held to his lips the hand she had offered him.

"Good Lord, how kind of you!" he finally managed to say.

"No, but I don't forget my friends, and I was worried."

She looked him full in the face, with that first searching glance by which a woman takes everything in, penetrates every thought to its roots, and brushes away every excuse. She must have been satisfied with the result, for her face lit up with a new smile. "It's nice, your hermitage here. Are you happy in it?"

"No, madame."

"Can it be possible? In this lovely country, in this beautiful forest, on this charming little river? But you must be at peace and quite happy here."

"No, madame."

"Why not?"

"Because of what I cannot forget."

"And is it indispensable that you forget something in order to be happy?"

"Yes, madame."

"May I know what it is?"

"You do know."

"And then...?"

"Then I am quite miserable."

With a pitying complacency, she said, "I guessed as much when I got your telegram, which is why I came. I had decided to leave immediately if I was mistaken." After a brief silence, she added: "Since I'm not leaving immediately, might I be given a tour of your... property? There's a little path between the lindens over there that looks delightful. Surely we'd be cooler there than here in this room."

They went outdoors. She was wearing a mauve dress which suddenly harmonized so completely with the foliage of the trees and the blue sky that she looked amazingly like an apparition, lovely and seductive in a new and unexpected way. Her long supple waist, her delicate fresh face, the little blond flame of her hair under a broad mauve hat which was encircled by a long ostrich feather, her slender arms, her hands holding her rolled umbrella in front of her, and her rather upright bearing, somewhat detached and proud, brought something abnormal, unexpected, exotic into this little country garden, the bizarre and delicious sensation of a storybook figure or a Watteau painting that a poet's imagination or a painter's whim had brought into the country just to demonstrate how lovely she was.

Staring at her with the deep exhalation of his entire returning passion, Mariolle remembered the two figures glimpsed on the road to Montigny.

She asked him, "Who is that little person who let me into your house?"

"My servant."

"She doesn't look... like a servant."

"No. She's extremely nice."

"Where did you find her?"

"Quite near here, in a sort of artists' hotel where the clients were threatening her virtue."

"Which you saved?"

He blushed, and answered, "Which I saved."

"To your advantage, perhaps?"

"To my advantage certainly, for as you know I prefer seeing pretty faces around me to ugly ones."

"And is that the only feeling she inspires in you?"

"She may have inspired me with an irresistible need to see you again, for any woman I like to look at, even for a second, makes me think of you."

"That's a very skillful answer which you just made up. Does she love her savior?"

He blushed more deeply. In a flash, the conviction that all jealousy is stimulant for a woman's heart made him decide to lie only by halves, and so he answered, hesitating, "I really don't know. It's possible. She's very attentive and takes good care of me."

An almost imperceptible annoyance made Madame de Burne murmur, "And you...?"

He looked at her, his eyes glowing with love, and said, "Nothing could distract me from you."

This too was very skillful, but she no longer noticed, so much did this sentence seem to her the expression of an indisputable truth. Could a woman like her doubt such a thing? She did not doubt it, as a matter of fact, and quite content now, no longer concerned herself with Élisabeth.

They sat down on two canvas chairs in the shade of the lindens, overlooking the rushing little stream.

Then he asked, "What could you have thought of me?"

"That you were very unhappy."

"Was that my fault or yours?"

"It was our fault."

"And then?"

"And then, realizing how upset you were, how overwrought, I decided that the most sensible thing I could do was first of all to let you calm down. So I waited."

"What did you wait for?"

"Some word from you. Which I received, and here I am. Now we are going to talk like serious people. So: you still love me? I am not asking you that as a coquette, I'm asking you that as a friend."

"I still love you."

"And what are your intentions?"

"How do I know? I'm in your hands."

"Oh, I . . . I have some very clear and distinct ideas, but I'm not telling you what they are without hearing yours. Tell me about you, about what has been going on in your heart and in your mind since you . . . escaped."

"I've thought about you, I haven't done much else."

"Yes, but how—in what sense? To what end?"

He told her of his determination to be cured of her, his flight, his arrival in this great forest where he had found nothing but her, his days pursued by the memory of her, his nights consumed by jealousy; he told everything, in complete good faith, except the love of Élisabeth, whose name he never mentioned again.

Madame de Burne listened to him, confident that he was not lying, convinced by the sense of her power over him even more than by the sincerity of his voice, and delighted by her triumph and her recovery of him, for she really was, after all, very fond of him.

Then he lamented this hopeless situation and, excited by speaking of what he had suffered for so long, he reproached her again, with impassioned lyricism but without anger, without bitterness, dismayed and overwhelmed by her incapacity to love, which was her curse. Over and over he insisted: "Others lack the talent to please; you are denied the talent to love . . ."

She interrupted him with sudden animation, overflowing with arguments and rationalizations. "At least I have the talent of being faithful. Would you be less miserable if, after adoring you for ten months, I was in love today with someone else?"

He exclaimed, "Then is it impossible for a woman to love only one man?"

"A woman cannot always love," she answered quickly, "she can only be faithful. And do you imagine that the exalted delirium of the senses can last for years on end? No, no. As for the majority of women given to passions, to violent liaisons lasting . . . however long they last, such women merely live their lives as a novel: the heroes differ, the circumstances and the crises change, the outcomes vary. For such women it must be diverting, even entertaining, for the feelings at the start, in the middle, and at the end are different each time. But for the man, when it's over, it's over. Do you understand?"

"Yes, I suppose I do. But I don't see what you're driving at."

"At this: there are no passions which last very long, I mean burning, tormenting passions of the sort you're still suffering. It's a phase which I've made painful, very painful for you, I know that now, by the... aridity of my kind of tenderness, by my incapacity for... expansion. But this phase passes, it can't go on indefinitely—" She broke off.

He asked anxiously, "And then?"

"And then I believe that for a reasonable and calm woman like myself, you can become a most agreeable lover, for you have a great deal of tact. On the other hand you'd be a dreadful husband. But no other kind exists, there are no good husbands."

Surprised and a little offended, he asked, "Why keep a lover you don't love, or one you no longer love?"

She answered sharply, "I love in my own way, my friend. I love drily, but I love."

"Above all, you need to be loved," he sighed with resignation, "and you need your lover to show it."

"Yes, that's true. I adore that. But my heart also needs a secret companion. That vainglorious need for public homage doesn't keep me from being devoted and faithful, and from believing I can give a man something intimate no one else could have: my loyal affection, my heart's sincere attachment, my soul's absolute and secret confidence. And in return I can receive from him, with all his lover's tenderness, the rare and delicious impression that I am not altogether alone. I know this is not love as you understand it, but it is worth something!"

He leaned toward her, trembling with emotion, and stammered, "Would you like me to be that man?"

"Yes, a little later, when you're not suffering so much. Meanwhile, be resigned to suffering a little, from me, now and then. It will pass. Since you're going to suffer in any case, it's better to do so near me than far away, isn't it?"

Her smile seemed to be saying, "Trust me a little," and since she could see that he was trembling with passion, she felt throughout her whole body a sort of well-being, a satisfaction which made her happy in her own way, the way a sparrow hawk is happy to plummet down upon her fascinated prey.

"When will you come back?" she asked.

"When? Why...tomorrow."

"Fine, tomorrow. You'll have dinner with me?"

"Yes, madame."

"And now I must be going," she said, glancing at the tiny clock concealed in the handle of her umbrella.

"Oh—why so soon?"

"Because I'm catching the five o'clock train. I'm giving a little dinner tonight—Princess von Malten, Bernhaus, Lamarthe, Massival, Maltry, and a newcomer, Monsieur de Charlaine, the explorer who's just back from Upper Cambodia after a remarkable journey. There's a lot of talk about him just now."

Mariolle felt a sudden pang. All those names, one after the other, were painful to him, like so many wasp stings. They contained poison. "In that case," he said, "shall we start now and take a drive through the forest?"

"I'd love that. But give me some tea and toast before we leave."

When the tea was ready, Élisabeth was not to be found. "She must be out doing errands," the cook said. Madame de Burne was not surprised. And indeed what apprehension could this servant afford her? In a few moments they got into the landau waiting at the door, and Mariolle had the driver take the longer route through the Gorge aux Loups. As they rolled along under the cool shade of the enormous green vault, accompanied by countless nightingales at this hour of the afternoon, Madame de Burne, moved by the mysterious beauty of this natural world, exclaimed, "Lord, how wonderful it is here—so lovely, so peaceful!" She sighed with the happy relief of a shriven sinner filled with languor and tender yearning. She rested her hand on André's.

But he thought, "Ah yes, nature—just like Mont-Saint-

Michel," and before his eyes passed a vision of a train leaving for Paris. He was taking her to the station. When she left him she said, "Till tomorrow, eight o'clock."

"Till tomorrow, madame, eight o'clock." She left him then, smiling radiantly, and he returned to his villa in the landau, satisfied, indeed happy, but still troubled, for nothing was resolved.

Yet why struggle? It was of no use. She cast a spell over him which he could not fathom, a spell stronger than ever. There was no escaping her, and separation was merely an intolerable privation, while if he could resign himself a little, he would have at least as much of her as she had promised him, for she never lied.

The horses trotted along under the trees, and he thought that during their entire time together, she had not once had an impulse to kiss him, to let him kiss her. She was just the same. Nothing would ever change in her, and always, perhaps, he would suffer at her hands in the same way. The memory of the bad times he had already endured, with the intolerable certainty that he could never change her, sent another pang through his heart, and made him dread the tribulations to come and the comparable distresses of the future. Yet he was resigned to suffer everything rather than lose her once more, resigned to that eternal desire which in his veins had turned to a sort of savage, unappeasable thirst that consumed his flesh.

Those rages so often endured on his way home alone after the times at Auteuil were beginning again, his body was already trembling in the landau rolling under the cool shade of the great trees, when suddenly the thought of Élisabeth waiting for him, cool too and young and pretty, her heart full of love and her mouth full of kisses, spread a kind of appeasement in his heart. Soon he would hold her in his arms, and with his eyes closed, deceiving himself as one deceives others, combining in the intoxication of the embrace the one he loved and the one by whom he was loved, he would possess them both. Yes, even now he longed for her, for that that grateful attachment of body and soul, that sensation of inspired tenderness and shared pleasure which always moves the human animal. Would this darling child not be, for his parching soul, the little spring found at the end of the day, the hope of cool water that sustains a man's energy crossing the desert?

But when he was back in his villa, the girl had not returned and he was alarmed, anxious, and said to the other servant, "You're sure she left?"

"Yes, monsieur."

Then he left too, hoping to meet her. When he had taken a few steps before turning into the road that climbs the length of the valley, he saw in front of him the wide, low structure of the old church with its stubby steeple, crouching on a little hill and sheltering, as a hen guards her chicks, the houses of its little village.

A suspicion, a presentiment, moved him to go in. Who knows the strange divinations of a woman's heart? What had she thought? What had she understood? Where had she taken refuge if not here, once the shadow of the truth had passed before her eyes?

The church was very dark, for it was already evening. Only the little lamp dangling on the end of its wire revealed, in the tabernacle, the Divine Consoler's presence. Mariolle walked quickly past the pews. When he reached the choir, he made out a woman on her knees, her face in her hands. He approached her, recognized her, touched her shoulder. They were alone. She started violently as she turned her head. She was crying.

"What is the matter?" he asked.

She murmured, "I know what it is. You're here because she's made you unhappy. She came to take you away."

Moved by the pain he had caused in his turn, he stammered, "You're mistaken, my child. I am going back to Paris, that's true, but I'm taking you with me."

Incredulously, she repeated, "You're not, you're not!"

"I swear to you I am."

"When?"

"Tomorrow."

Beginning to sob again, she moaned, "Oh my God! My God!" Then he put an arm around her waist, raised her to her feet, led her away, and together they walked down the little hill into the shadows of the evening; and when they were on the riverbank, he made her sit down in the grass and sat beside her. He could feel her heart beating and hear her choked breathing, and overcome by remorse, he pressed her to him, whispering the tender words he had never spoken to her before. Moved by pity and burning with desire, he was scarcely lying and certainly not deceiving her; and he wondered, surprised at what he was saying and what he was feeling, how, still responding to the presence of the other woman who had enslaved him forever, he could thrill this way with desire and emotion even as he consoled these pangs of love.

He promised to love her dearly—he did not quite say "to love her"—and to provide her, at his side, with a fine home suitable for a lady, with pretty furniture and a maid to serve her.

She grew calmer as she listened to him, gradually reassured, incapable of believing that he was tricking her by his words, understanding, moreover, from the way he spoke them that he was sincere. Convinced at last and dazzled by the vision of being a lady in her turn, by this dream of a child born so poor, a servant at the inn, suddenly the mistress of a man so rich and so fine, she was intoxicated with longing, with gratitude, and with pride, all of which mingled in her attachment for André. Flinging her arms around his neck, she stammered, as she covered his face with kisses, "I love you so much! There's nothing except you inside me."

And he returned her caresses as he murmured, deeply touched, "Dear, dear little girl."

Already she had almost completely forgotten the apparition of that stranger which had caused her so much grief. Yet a kind of unconscious doubt still floated in her mind, and she asked in her coaxing voice, "Truly, you'll love me... like here?"

He answered confidently, "I'll love you like here."

TITLES IN SERIES

For a complete list of titles, visit www.nyrb.com or write to:
Catalog Requests, NYRB, 435 Hudson Street, New York, NY 10014